Four Walls

Sade Josephine

authorHOUSE®

AuthorHouse™
1663 Liberty Drive
Bloomington, IN 47403
www.authorhouse.com
Phone: 1 (800) 839-8640

Published by AuthorHouse 02/09/2018

ISBN: 978-1-5462-2814-1 (sc)
ISBN: 978-1-5462-2813-4 (e)

Library of Congress Control Number: 2018901638

Print information available on the last page.

Any people depicted in stock imagery provided by Getty Images are models, and such images are being used for illustrative purposes only. Certain stock imagery © Getty Images.

This book is printed on acid-free paper.

Because of the dynamic nature of the Internet, any web addresses or links contained in this book may have changed since publication and may no longer be valid. The views expressed in this work are solely those of the author and do not necessarily reflect the views of the publisher, and the publisher hereby disclaims any responsibility for them.

For everyone who had a random idea and didn't know what to do with it.

Author's Note

Among the many traits that make up a person, I can elaborate on six important ones: desire, regret, trepidation, capitulation, sense of amusement, and euphoria.

- Desire; Every human being has a desire for something. There's always something that makes someone happy and doesn't make them agitated when they have to do it over and over again.
- Regret; Once in awhile, someone, no matter what their age, lie awake thinking one of the most common questions "why didn't I do that when I had the chance?"
- Trepidation; Trepidation is just another word for paranoia, fearing the possibility that something you want to happen won't happen and that something you don't want to happen will.
- Capitulation; The ability to cave under pressure comes with every person. It blocks out desire when desire is still there. Every leader is a follower.

- Sense of amusement; Humor is the only thing that can keep a person sane during serious circumstances.
- Euphoria; Happiness allows us to love the life that we are given.

This is a story about six different girls who needed each other more than they realized as they each find themselves. They are all the same because they are all different. Without their experiences within the confinements of their collided worlds, they would have been stuck in a life they weren't familiar with because of how different it was from the lives they dreamed of having. Those lives showed what their interests were and what they wanted to be, which, whether they knew it or not, was the first step to finding out who they really are.

Many parents think that children finding out who they are is just something that happens in an instant. And it could happen. But sometimes denial clouds judgement. So even if a person knows they're living a lie--a lie buried deep beneath the surface of their perception of reality so that no one can find it--they still don't believe they are.

I think the beautiful thing about stories are that no matter how hard you try to muster or create something from the realm of your imagination, there are segments that could actually be happening at this very moment in a different part of the world. This could be a true story if you want it to be.

One

I've learned that people will forget what you said, people will forget what you did, but people will never forget how you made them feel.

• Maya Angelou

"What are you watching?" Bleu skillfully removed her blonde curls out of her boyfriend's oversized black and yellow varsity jacket with a single swoop of her hand after she put it on. Eden, sitting back against the olive green couch, didn't take her eyes off of the large 60 inch flat screen. Her coily light ginger curls dangling in front of her face, didn't waver from its stagnant glower at the TV screen.

"Do the Right Thing."

"I think I heard of it," Bleu said. "What's it about?"

Eden sighed. "How frustrating stimuli can stimulate people into letting their biased perspectives affect their judgement and how white people are able to get away with *everything*. Something like that at least." The volume of the TV speakers augmented when Spike Lee sent a trash can hurling into the glass window of a pizzeria.

Bleu stood frozen in shock. "Oh."

Eden looked over at Bleu while she was watching the TV screen and then back at the TV.

"Where's Mercury?" Thats me. I'm Mercury.

"Bathroom," Eden replied.

"Ah." She fit her hands into her pocket and awkwardly tapped her foot. "Oh wait." She headed into the kitchen. Eden sighed again. She delicately played with the end of her loose curl, stretching it down. She watched it bounce back up whenever she let go of it. Bleu returned with her notorious self assured stride holding a neatly rolled up piece of paper in her hand. "Here. Happy Birthday."

Eden opened up the paper. I couldn't get a good look at the picture from where I was hiding. Her eyes lit up like time-lapsed roses. "Woah. Bleu, you drew this? It looks just like Maya Angelou."

"I painted it, actually." Bleu smiled. She nervously clutched the elbow of her arm behind her back. Eden's probably the only person Bleu would act like a complete sycophant around. "It took me two days."

"Sweet." Eden looked up with a polite grin and raised the paper up. "Thank you."

"You're welcome." She cleared her throat and looked over by the hallway where I was standing. I quickly darted behind the wall before she caught sight of me. A car horn honked outside.

A draft of cold air blew in when Bleu opened the front door. I peeked behind the wall again. "Where are you going?" Eden asked.

"To a party." I scoffed. When is she not typical?

"Someone else's birthday?" Eden asked. She laughed but I knew she was hurt.

2

"It's just a celebratory thing." Bleu shrugged. "For our school team winning the football game."

"Oh yeah," Eden said her voice trailing off. "I heard about that."

Bleu started swinging her keys around her index finger as she poked her cheek out with her tongue. "Um you can come if you want." This girl is trying to take my friend away from me.

Eden narrowed her eyes at her sister. "Uhh no thanks. I'm kind of tired. Maybe Mercury and I will order a pizza or something." She focused back on the TV.

"Bleu, let's go!" I know that voice. It's that other bitchy girl from my school, Cassidy. Every Monday she checks my homework to copy off of it before Math starts.

"I'm coming!" Bleu shouted back. She leaned against the couch so that she was the same height as Eden. "Listen, Eden," she spoke condescendingly. "It's not healthy to have a friend who can't say anything back."

My heart began beating really fast. She got me.

Eden turned to face her.Whatever, Bleu." Then she laughed and said in a lower voice, "At least I have real friends."

Bleu scoffed. "'Whatever' is right. Lock the door behind me." She slammed it closed.

I slowly came out from behind the wall. Eden smiled at me sympathetically.

"She's an asshole, okay?" She patted the empty space on the couch beside her.

It's true. I can't talk. I have selective mutism which is a speech disorder that doesn't allow me to talk in situations where I don't feel comfortable. My friend Eden's been really supportive about it. She's been calling me The Little Mermaid referencing the princess that couldn't speak on land.

I don't know.

Even though she's my best friend, I know she's getting sick and tired of me not being able to say anything to her. Like when she talks about her crush, Yusuf, and how she gets so hyped when she babbles on about him. If it's not his hair, it's his face, and if it's not his face it's his cute little freckles that resemble constellations. Her words not mine.

It's easy to see that she wants me to say something of more substance than what I write out in the little black notebook I carry with me everywhere. Usually I say things like, "He's nice" or "He does have nice eyes, I guess". I never really understood what it was about him that she liked. There's no hype. I mean, clearly I wouldn't be able to figure it out, but in general the guy is just plain. When he speaks, it's one word answers every time. I'm sure between the two of us, I'm the one that has a more embellished outlook on things. Meaning, I guarantee you that I say a lot more than he does in my head. Eden's infatuation wasn't going to be stopped by the likes of me. She's too deep into this now.

The next day, we went out to eat at this diner she works at called Mary's Diner. She was off work that day but they make the best pancakes in our town. It was quiet when we ate. Kind of like all the other times we've eaten there in the past two years, but this time was different. This time, it was awkward and it's never awkward. I felt awful. I was seeing my best friend slowly start to realize she lost two years of her life that could've been spent with someone who would have the confidence to say something. It feels like that sometimes. Like I don't have the confidence.

I'm sure she's confused about why this happened to me so abruptly and how quickly her life changed because of such a small alteration in our lives. I watched her sip the decaf coffee she ordered while staring out the window at a woman tying her poodle to a tree. Eden felt my eyes on her and looked over in my direction with a frown. She set her drink down. "What's wrong?"

I opened my mouth to speak but nothing could come out. My face felt hot with embarrassment and I felt like I was gonna cry. I looked at the napkin on my lap.

"Uh...Hold that thought." She stood up quickly from the booth. "I have to pee. I'll be right back." She paced off behind me to the restroom.

I covered my face with my hands digging my nails into my skin.

"Want a refill on your Sprite?"

I looked up towards the deep soothing voice. It was Quincy. Her hair was in extensions, curly black to blonde curls which contrasted well with her coffee brown skin. She was wearing a bright yellow pineapple printed Hawaiian t-shirt and beige cargo shorts under her green apron. I shook my head with a polite smile. Quincy ruffled my thick pink hair softly.

"Okay, girl."

Quincy's on my soccer team at my high school, Emerald High. She's a senior. She's gay, like me, and nice so I like her. But I don't like her like that even though she's a massive flirt. She's really cute, though. She's the co-captain of the soccer team because the coach couldn't figure out who was a better player between her and Bleu. Every time they played against each other there was a stalemate. Bleu, Eden's half sister, hates Quincy. Bleu hates everyone that poses as a threat to her. Quincy hates her back and she doesn't care about what Bleu or her snobby friends think which is another

5

corny reason why I like her. The whole reason why Bleu hates Quincy was because back in 8th grade Quincy did an interpretive dance and won the talent show. She beat Bleu who timidly sung Toxic by Britney Spears.

Eden sat back down in front of me but I already wrote a note in my notebook. ***I have to go home. My dad just texted me.***

"Oh okay. Want me to drive you?"

I shook my head and headed out. My dad never texted me but I couldn't look at her without feeling sorry for myself anymore.

That night, I became aware that the breakfast incident affected her as much as it affected me. Eden climbed into my bedroom and crawled under my comforter. Her feet were freezing. We became best friends because of how close our houses were together. Our roofs were placed underneath our windows, overlapping one another. When we were little, we would jump onto each other's balconies late at night if we had a bad dream. I shut my eyes, until all I could see was a deep shade of red, pretending to be fast asleep.

"Mercury?"

I kept my eyes closed. I even gave out a fake tiny snore.

She tucked a strand of my pink hair behind my ear. Her arm wrapped around my middle and tucked her chilled feet in between my legs as she dug her head into my back. I could smell the fruity scent of her shampoo. My eyes began to flutter. A part of me wanted to see her while the remainder of myself tried to calm down.

"I wish you would talk to me," she whispered.

Two

In your life, you meet people. Some you never think about again. Some, you wonder what happened to them. There are some that you wonder if they ever think about you. And then there are some you wish you never had to think about again. But you do.

•   C.S Lewis

Bleu's mother died a maternal death when delivering her and her twin, Todd. Then Bleu's father met Eden's mother. Eden's mother was black which is why Eden is obviously black. Eden's mother practically became Bleu's mother before Eden was born so they were equally upset when she passed away with leukemia when we were in seventh grade.

Ever since then, Bleu is the type of person that you wouldn't be able to see with your own two eyes. There are layers to Bleu so that you don't see what she really enjoys or what she thinks about almost anything. Bleu was like an onion.

She's in a relationship with a boy named Stuart. The only time I see her smile is when she's with him. With her lips at least. Her eyes have been dead for a while now. I think her smile is just for publicity. Publicity is a funny word for it.

7

I don't know. Her smile just doesn't seem genuine.

I'm just thinking about Bleu. She used to be fun.

Bleu shoved past Jasmine and I as she cut the lunch line. Jasmine's another girl in my grade but I don't know her that well. "Move," Bleu said harshly.

Jasmine's apple rolled off the tray and onto the floor. Bleu and another bitch named Rachel smiled complacently with one another. They both entered their pin numbers at the register and went back to their lunch table basking in their stress free lives. Jasmine's olive skin faintly blushed pink.

"I feel like someone tried to get the stick out of her ass but it broke off and now it's just stuck up in there," Eden said next to us.

I snorted as I collected my lunch. The lunch lady snorted, too.

"You know my brother got laid last night and I heard the whole thing," Eden whispered.

My eyes widened.

"I mean," she scoffed. "Even though, Todd is one of the most exasperating pestilential beings I have ever stumbled upon, I still tolerate him more than Bleu." She picked up Jasmine's apple off the floor. "But both of them are completely ignorant to the concept of having the ability to exude basic human decency."

Jasmine, entering her pin number, laughed wholeheartedly. Eden turned to look at Jasmine. "Am I wrong?"

Jasmine smirked and shook her head. "Not at all." She paid for her lunch and left.

"I like her," Eden said pointing to her with the apple. "She's never had a bad hair day." She pointed to her head.

I swatted her arm roughly.

"Ow! What? It's true. Wish I had me one of those things."

A hijab? I wrote.

"Whatever," she said. "I like it."

—

"Pass me the damn ball, Quincy!"

Quincy glared at Bleu while also trying to focus on the goal ahead. I was squinting from the goal net on the opposite side of the field trying to see Quincy's steal. Quincy accelerated her speed and kicked the ball straight into the goal with great vigor, the crowd erupted into cheers. Quincy looked back over at Bleu and shrugged modestly. Bleu stuck her middle finger up in her direction. I sprinted over to Quincy, struggling to get to her past my excited reeling teammates who were perspiring like crazy with grass stuck to their white uniforms. I tackled her down to the ground overwhelmed with happiness if only for a second. Quincy ruffled my pink hair.

The referee blew her whistle. "Hawks win the game!" That's us. We're the Hawks.

The team made it into the locker room with their gold medals, prattling about what they wish they would have done to each of the opposing teammates that pissed them off. Personally, I really wanted to sucker punch the girl with the blue bandana who kicked me in the shin for nothing since she couldn't make the goal in.

Cassidy came up to Quincy and I in the locker room. "Lucky shot," she said in a monotone voice before heading back over to the girls.

I wrote in my notepad: ***That means thanks for winning the game.***

9

Quincy laughed. "It's whatever. I'll take it."

I reached into my locker and pulled out my white hand towel to wipe myself off. I turned around and noticed Quincy trying to use her inhaler discreetly.

"Like you ran enough," Bleu scoffed.

Her abrupt appearance made us both jump. Quincy quickly hid the inhaler behind her back hitting her hand back against the locker with a bang. "God." She clutched her hands together in pain. Bleu's eyes softened. She pretended she didn't see anything and headed back over to her friends by the showers. Quincy was completely unfazed by Bleu's sudden transformation in her demeanor. She pulled out the inhaler again and took the air in.

I wrote out on my note pad, *Thanks for winning the game.*

Quincy wrapped me in a sweaty hug.

"Quincy!"

She slowly released me from the hug and looked at a bubbly Asian girl wide eyed with long shimmery black hair in a ponytail cascading down her back. She was wearing our team colors, black and yellow, on her cheerleading uniform.

"I saw the game," she said smiling like crazy. "Congratulations. You were great."

"Eh." Quincy shrugged and winked over at me. "It was nothing. Hey are you still considering joining the team?"

I quizzically studied her body language while she was talking to her. Her leg was up on the wooden bench. She was biting her lip and looking up at the girl from underneath her eyelashes.

"Yeah but it's a little too late now. Besides I prefer

chccrleading more anyway. I get to see you play and not worry about getting knocked on my ass."

"You like seeing me play?"

The girl shrugged with a cocky smile. "Yeah I kinda do."

My eyes widened. It's like I wasn't even there.

I was air. Nevertheless, I took that as my cue to leave. But of course, I forgot my towel. I realized this as I was walking back home. Quincy and the girl were still in the locker room and it was already eight o'clock. I caught a familiar blonde standing outside the front door of the locker room with a phone held up. She heard me make my way over and her eyes widened. Nonchalantly, I glanced down at her phone. It was recording the noises coming out of the locker room. Bleu and I shared an awkward gaze. I attempted to snatch up her phone but she held it up higher. Unbelievable. I reached for my notebook.

"Don't bother. I don't want to read what you have to say."

I furiously shoved her out of the way and went to the door.

"Great," she said. "Interrupt them. They'll be thrilled."

I bit my lip and wrote something on the notebook.

"What are you doing?" she asked.

I stuck my tongue out at her and opened the door. The Asian girl screamed the instant she saw me and covered herself up. Quincy stood up instantly pulling her pants up. "Mercury what ar-"

I showed her my notebook. ***Bleu's recording you guys.*** Quincy's eyes enlarged. "Shit." She sprinted out the locker room with only a bra and the uniform shorts on. I hastily followed behind her. Bleu was racing across the gymnasium at lightning speed but Quincy was faster. She caught her by her ponytail.

"Give it to me."

"Give what?" Blue asked.

"Give it here now, Evans!" She pulled her ponytail down roughly making Bleu wince. She gave in and handed the large smartphone over to her.

Quincy deleted the voice recording, handed her her phone and pushed her away. "God, you really are something else, aren't you? I'm not even pissed I just feel sorry for your sick ass."

"For me? Don't waste your time." She headed for the door.

"You took the words right out of my mouth." Bleu turned around but Quincy was already jogging back to the lockers.

Three

We all know we have a finite period of time. I just feel if I'm going to be alive, I want to be challenged - to be as immortal as possible. The path to that isn't an easy way, but it's a rewarding way.

- **Frank Ocean**

I was raised by three boys. My dad, my brother and this kid named William Monteith who I've known since I was 4. He's the guy that was fortunately there to save my life. But that's another story. I've always been fascinated by William's ability to be happy with everything. Even with my brother, Zachariah, Z for short, who is a personified Debbie downer. They've been "best friends" most of their lives. God forbid I call them anything else. Zachariah is the definition of the average American teenage white boy. He's got the gelled-into-a-style dyed blond hair, girlfriend on his arm, friends who laugh at jokes he makes that don't have to be funny, he smokes weed once a week without worrying about getting caught, and he used to go to parties, like the ones Bleu goes to, back when he was in high school. William is the stereotypical American teenage black boy:

seen as looking for trouble when he's not, one girl a month, practices basketball every day, makes jokes white people can't laugh at, and acts tough even when he feels like he's not. Zachariah and William are both the manliest men you'll ever come across.

Last Friday, William raced to my bedroom door out of breath in his plain white boxers. He gripped the door frame. The second he caught his breath he said. "Where's your brother?"

I sat up frowning at him. He was supposed to be vacationing in St. Lucia.

"I'm leaving for my vacation in ten minutes," he said reading the look on my face. "C'mon where is he?" I jumped out of the bed. Eden, who was sitting beside me, looked at me confused. She always comes over before soccer practice every Friday. I dashed over to the railing. Scanning my eyes over the first floor, I pointed to Z making out with his girlfriend, Sydney on the couch.

"Can I borrow these?" He grabbed the store bought bag of red grapes out of my hands. I was so content in seeing him that I just watched with glee as he started chucking them at Z. He missed the first two tries and then got him square in the face. The grape bounced off his forehead and onto Sydney's lap.

"Ow!" Z peered upward grimacing. William quickly ducked in time and stifled a laugh. Z's eyes landed on me.

"What the fuck, Mercury?"

I waved him up.

"I'm busy right now," he said aggravated. "Can it wait?"

I shook my head.

Sydney rolled her eyes as Z headed upstairs to meet

me. Once he was at the top step, out of sight of Sydney, he said, "What is it, Merc-" William clamped his hand over Z's mouth and lifted him up off the ground. I giggled from the look on Z's face. William threw him into his room. He closed the door behind them laughing.

Smiling like a dopey idiot, I went back into my room.

"What the hell was that about?" Eden asked. "Was that William Monteith?"

I got out a piece of paper from my wooden desk drawer and wrote: **What do you think?**

"Okay one: the hostility? I can do without. And two: holy shit you never told me about this."

I know, I wrote.

"Poor, Sydney…" she said. I nodded suddenly reluctant about my excitement with the whole ordeal. My heart started beating like an approaching motorcycle the second I caught Sydney coming up the stairs.

"Uh oh," Eden said for me.

Without a single thought in my head, I raced out of the room and stood in front of Sydney.

"Where's Z?"

Eden ran out of my bedroom passing both Sydney and I and vehemently knocked on his bedroom door. She tentatively turned to face her.

"Can I see what he's doing please?"

I shook my head. One day she'll thank me for this.

"You're so…" She laughed bitterly and moved past me.

Eden slammed on the door with her palms before Sydney gently passive aggressively pushed her away.

The door swung open. "Okay okay Mercury I got it. Is

this what you wanted?" He handed me a brown paper bag. He frowned at Sydney. "Oh, what are you doing upstairs?"

Sydney peeked into his room. "Nothing."

Eden bit her tongue trying not to laugh unfortunately making me give out a small one. Sydney glared at the two of us. Z wrapped his arm around Sydney and descended down the staircase. He winked back at Eden and I.

Eden let all her nervous giggles out. I exaggeratedly wrapped my arm around her like Z did to Sydney. She snorted and pushed me away. "What's in the bag?" She asked.

I opened it and inside was a tube of toothpaste.

"Brilliant."

The two of us hesitantly looked inside Z's room and sure enough there was William out of breath staring up at the ceiling. His chest rhythmically heaving up and down.

Tears prickled Z's eyes and rolled down his red freckled cheeks. "You can laugh, asshole."

"I'm not gonna laugh," William said.

"Fine," Z wiped his eyes with his yellow sleeve. "But you can."

William rolled his eyes. "I'm not gonna laugh." He glanced down at his watch.

"Fine!"

"Fine!"

"Flush it."

"Are you sure?" William looked over at me for reassurance. I shrugged.

"Just do it, bastard!" Z ordered.

William flared his nostrils angrily. He peered down at the bobbing goldfish in the toilet bowl.

"Will!" He urged. William flushed the toilet and watched the goldfish slowly swirl down.

Z rested his head against the cold porcelain seat. His tears dropped one by one to the white tile floor.

"You're such a faggot you know that?" William frowned. "Crying over a fish. Sure it's funny as hell but it's so sad how pathetic you are. How pathetic you've become is mind blowing." He stood up off the cold bathroom tiles and walked out of the bathroom. I followed suit.

"You're the faggot, faggot." Z folded his arms over his chest.

William glared at him. I looked between the both of them during their staring contest that seemed to last five minutes. "I'm going to pretend I didn't hear that."

"You're the faggot not me."

"Hey!" William turned around startling Z. He pointed a finger in his face. "You better shut up or I won't hesitate to beat the shit out of you." He headed over to Z's window he initially climbed in from.

"You can't beat the shit out of me. Y-you you c-couldn't hurt me if you t-tried."

William cackled. "Oh y-yeah," he said mocking his stuttering. "You wanna bet."

Z nodded fervently appearing strangely pleased. "Yeah, bet."

William turned around and slapped Z hard across the face.

I gasped. There was a loud ringing in my ears almost as if he slapped me too. I didn't think he was actually going to do it. "Is that it?" Z asked.

William slapped him again.

Z visibly tried not to cry from the pain. "No, man," he

jumped up and down. *"I want you to beat the shit out of me. Get out of here Mercury. You're making him soft."*

"Okay," William said. *Z closed his eyes and waited for the blow. William glanced over at me with an amused grin and put a finger to his lips. I nodded. I wasn't sure what he was planning on doing but whatever it was, I was excited about it. He always had something fascinating in store.*

William put a bright red and white koi fish in a small knotted plastic bag on his nightstand and headed into the bathroom. He dampened a cloth before putting it to Z's red cheek. *"You should have bet money on it, white boy."*

Z didn't open his eyes. He only closed them tighter.

William and I didn't say anything. We looked at each other confused.

After a minute, Z opened his eyes and wrapped William's hand into a fist. *"Hit me. C'mon."*

William smiled smugly. *"Why? You were right."* *He headed over to the window.* *"See you tomorrow."*

Suddenly, Z socked William right in the jaw mercilessly causing him to nearly fall out the window.

"Z?!" *I exclaimed. I ran over to William.* *"Will, are you alright?"*

Will's mouth began to bleed profusely.

"Oh Will..." *Z backed up and blinked from his moderately remorseless trance. He gripped his hair not knowing what to do with himself.* *"I didn't...I didn't mean to..."*

I was furious. *"Z?! Why'd you do that?"*

"I-it was an accident. I was just c-caught up."

William shook his head. *"It's fine."* *But the bleeding didn't cease.*

"You just make me so mad," *Z declared. He balled his*

hands. *"You just make me so m-mad and you always, always gotta call me a faggot. I hate when you call me a faggot because you n-never apologize or say you're joking about it. It's like you mean it, Will."*

William tried to catch the blood dripping from his mouth.

Z looked over at his nightstand and spotted the fish in the clear plastic bag swimming around. "Just go. Here." He placed the washcloth to his mouth.

William immediately left through the window.

-

"You okay?" I asked William on our way home from my elementary school. William and Z had picked me up. William showed off the stitches on his gums when he removed the ice. "I gotta keep holding ice to it."

"I'm sorry," Z said.

"You better be."

Z sighed. "You can name the goldfish if you want," he said. "Since, technically, it's yours."

"Aight." William hummed. He pondered for a moment. "I like the name Juan."

"Juan?" Z asked. William nodded. "Juan it is."

William kicked a rock while they were walking sending it out into the road.

"You can even keep calling me a faggot," Z blurted out. "If you want."

Oh Z, I thought to myself. William stopped walking and narrowed his eyes. He clenched his fists and held them at his sides. "What's it going to take for you to get it? Because I ain't ever gonna say it." He stared down at him intimidatingly. "No amount of money in the world is gonna make me say it. Not even if I knew I was dying the next day. Or if today was my last day on Earth. In fact, I'm never, ever going to say it. Ever. And I'll bet money on that believe me."

Z's face lit up like a fire was burning beneath his cheeks. "I get it."

"You don't get nothing." William smiled. "You're. Never. Going. To. Understand. Me. Zachariah." He poked his chest with each word.

"Just for that," Z, said standing taller. "I'm changing the fish's name."

"To what?"

"To Yuu. Y-u-u. It's a Japanese based name meaning excellence. Japan is known for their koi fish which is what you bought me. I hope Yuu isn't too unsettling."

"No. Not unsettling. Maybe stupid."

"Good. I love Yu."

William froze stiff.

"I really love Yu."

I bit my lip trying not to laugh. William seemed unfazed by Z's cringeworthy confession. He stared at him longingly. "Really?"

"Yeah." Z couldn't even look at him because of how red his face became. He gripped my arm. "C'mon, Mercury."

"Z," I said staring at his cheeks. "I think you're having an allergic reaction again."

"Shut up, c'mon." He pushed his red beanie down some more to hide his face and pulled my arm.

William stopped in front of his house while Z pushed me forward. I glanced behind me, confused to what just transpired, and saw pink pulsing heart eyes popping out of William's head.

Four

There are two conflicting philosophies that I love: "Everything happens for a reason," as well as "you can change everything that you have control over".

• Yara Shahidi

Bleu twisted the brass door knob open. "Hey..."

"Hi." The girl wearing a beige hijab and a long flowing white garment covering most of her skin fiddled with the end of her sleeve nervously.

"What's up?" Bleu chuckled humorlessly. She shifted onto one leg impatiently. "What are you doing at my house?"

"Oh um...you asked for tutoring. Calculus." Jasmine cleared her throat. "You gave your address in. See?" She showed her a piece of paper.

"Oh right. Right. Come in." She stepped out of the way so that she could pass through. Jasmine reluctantly stepped inside.

"So um, we can do this upstairs if that's cool with you?" Bleu asked.

"Sure." She caught sight of Eden and I on the couch.

A smile appeared across her face, relieved to see familiar friendly faces. "Oh, hey guys," she said. I waved.

Eden smiled. "Hey, Jas."

Mr. Evans, a tall man with a slim build and short cut blond hair resembling Bleu's, came from downstairs. He had large round shaped eye glasses perched on the bridge of his nose. "Bleu, who was at the door? Oh, hello."

Jasmine waved.

"This is Jasmine," Bleu said. "She's gonna help me with my math."

"Oh great. You girls hungry?"

"I'm okay," Jasmine said. "But thank you."

"We're good, Dad. Thanks." She headed upstairs with Jasmine.

"Um Bleu?" Her father said. He motioned her over with his finger. "Can I talk to you for a minute?"

Bleu bit her lip and came to a halt. "Uh my door's the first door on the right," she said to Jasmine. "You can just head in there if you want."

"Cool." Jasmine scurried up the steps probably excited to find out what Bleu was hiding in there. But I've been in her room. It's pretty dull. Not even one embarrassing pop star poster on the wall.

Bleu slumped down the steps to meet her father in the kitchen.

"He's an islamophobe," Eden whispered in my ear. She looked at me. "A big ignorant one."

My eyes widened. Eden's face contorted to make it look like she was in the middle of an unbearable stomach ache. "It's really embarrassing." She dug her hand into a bag of chips and ate it nervously until Bleu came out of the kitchen with a face so white it was nearly transparent. She jogged upstairs.

That's when I decided it was time to write to Eden. ***You don't have to be friends with me any more if you don't want to.***

Eden glanced down at the paper and stared at the words for a few minutes. Her hazel eyes flickered to meet mine. She whispered, "You don't have to be friends with *me*. I talk too damn much."

I can't even talk to you.

"Then what are you doing right now?"

Writing. You're not supposed to read over what I tell you. That's not how conversations work.

Eden rolled the page out, crumpled the paper up and threw it across the room. "There. Now that solves both of our problems." Eden smiled pleased with herself and leaned back on the couch to watch the rerun of A Different World. She reminded me of the character, Freddie Brooks because of her hair.

I felt like I overstayed my welcome at Eden's house so I left. Zachariah and William were still at home by themselves so I thought it'd be wise to just walk around the block for a few minutes to give them their space. As I was passing by Eden's house for what seemed like the third time, Jasmine stepped out and bounded down the stairs.

"Hey."

I pulled the black notebook out of my bag along with a pen. ***How was she?***

"Surprisingly okay. Is she usually mean consistently?"

You should be asking, Eden.

Jasmine laughed. "Good point."

"Hello." A boy our age with a swimmer's body wearing a Bulls jersey and beige cargo pants ran up to us.

"No," Jasmine said. She started walking away.

"What?" He appeared confused. "No?"

Jasmine stopped and turned around. "Why are you saying hi to me?" I was assuming she knew him.

"I just want to talk to you…"

"Because?" She asked seeming annoyed.

"Because I'm bored," He said looking over at me and then back at Jasmine.

"Because you're bored? You said hi to me because you were bored?"

"Yeah." He cleared his throat and shifted from side to side.

"Well I'm not alive to entertain you."

"You could be. No I mean-"

Jasmine's nostrils flared. "I'm gonna count to three. 1, 2-"

"Do you wanna hang out sometime?" He asked his voice cracking. I bit my lip trying to contain myself.

"I do not," Jasmine stated.

"Okay what can I do to make you wanna go out with me?"

"Nothing. 1-."

"Okay I can do nothing. I can do that."

"There's one thing you can do and I might consider."

The stars in his eyes lit up. "Yes?"

"Walk away and quit bugging me."

The boy instantly trailed off in the opposite direction. "How am I doing?!" He called out.

"You're doing well with the walking away part," Jasmine answered. "But you need some work on the second half."

He kept walking.

I wrote out on my notepad: *He's adorable.*

Jasmine shook her head. She turned around. The boy was waving with a hesitant grin plastered on his face.

Jasmine waved him back over with a sigh. He sprinted up to her. His brown hair whipping up and down.

A runner, I wrote.

"Hush." The boy appeared in front of her. "What's your name?" Oh, she didn't know him.

"Jack."

"I'm not into boys, Jack," she said. I'll admit, I got a tiny bit excited.

"Oh you're a lesbian?"

"No..."

"Oh I get it." He nodded. "You're into men not boys."

"I'm just into intimacy, actually."

I raised my eyebrows. Oh.

"Oh," Jack said. "Little Jack."

Jasmine nods.

"See, I really really like you but I'm not ready to get laid yet. Even though I really really like you."

"Who implied that they wanted to lay you down? Because it wasn't me."

Jack glanced over at me trying to see if *I* understood her. I bit my nails trying to hide my grin. I had no idea Jasmine could act this way. "I'm getting mixed signals."

"How are you getting mixed signals if you haven't even asked me out properly yet?" Jasmine asked.

"Well seeing how this is going," he said laughing awkwardly. "I'm not sure you'll give me the answer I want."

"You're just gonna give up? A'ight."

"Please go out with me," He blurted out.

"That's not a question."

"Can you please go out with me?" Jack begged.

"Why?" Jasmine asked.

"Because you're the prettiest girl I've ever met and I don't care if you're not my type I just like you and my friend told me that if I didn't ask you out then he would, just to spite me. Look at him. He's gorgeous." He pointed to the small pudgy Filipino kid with spiky black hair dribbling a basketball behind them.

"Sure. I'll go out with you."

"Oh thank god." He wrapped an arm around her shoulder and looked at the kid, motioning to Jasmine as he slowly bobbed his head up and down with a smile. "In your face, Levi." Jasmine and I began laughing.

The next day, I rode my skateboard to school without Eden. Even though we kind of cleared things up yesterday, I knew right then and there, she was worn out by me. "Hey, kid." William came up behind my bike and patted me on the back. He handed me a SpongeBob Squarepants printed gift-wrapped medium sized box. "This is for Z."

I stopped in my tracks and stuffed my skateboard in my bookbag. It was Z's 22nd birthday today.

"Give it to him when he's opening gifts in front of your family." He gave out his infamous wheezy laugh. "See you around."

Quincy stopped running. She wore a thick large afro now. The black coils highlighted by the sweat racing down her forehead. I paused beside her.

"Look Quincy," Bleu said as she jogged up to us. "I know being from another planet and everything makes it hard for you to take in our air but you've got to make some kind of effort." Her comment sent her friends into giggles.

"Very funny," she said weakly before placing her hands back on her knees and erupting into a wheezy fit.

Bleu and her friends continued their steady jog ahead of us. Without missing a beat, I went to fetch our coach pointing to Quincy who was resting on the grass hill.

The coach ran over to her with me following in tow. "Quincy, you alright?"

"I'm fine, it's just my asthma but my inhaler is empty." She shook her head. "I just need some water and I'll be fine." She gave a brave smile.

I raced to the sidewalk to get my unopened water bottle and came back over to them.

"Hey Quincy?" A ginger named June Matthews stopped jogging and looked down at Quincy. "Are you cool?"

Quincy nodded coughing. She took the offered bottle from me. "Thanks, kid."

I kneeled down beside her.

"Take it easy," June said causing Quincy's eyes to twinkle.

"Mercury, I didn't tell you to stop," Coach said. "Move it."

I got up off the grass and followed June's stride.

Quincy had to stay inside the entire time during practice. Coach said she could come out if she was up to it but I guess she never was. She was in the locker room still breathing kind of heavily when the team came back in.

"Nice hair, Quincy," Bleu said. Cassidy and Rachel stifled their laughter.

"Nice face, Bleu," Quincy countered. Most of the girls snickered.

"Nice life." The girls oohed. Everyone was staring now.

"Nice privilege."

"Thanks. I worked hard for it."

Quincy nodded. She got up and left the locker room with her blue Adidas duffle bag bouncing against her thigh. It got quiet.

Bleu rolled her eyes. "Some people take things too seriously." She roughly got her clothes out of her locker with an attitude. I resisted the urge to attack her. Instead I grabbed my things and roughly shoved past her on my way to Quincy.

"Watch it, Mars."

I stuck my middle finger up at her before slamming the door shut on my way out.

"Hey." Quincy was walking with her head down when I caught up with her. "I knew she hated me but I didn't know that's why she hated me. And I know it doesn't matter but isn't her sister black? I don't know it just took me aback, I guess." I wrapped my arm around her shoulders.

Z's friends left our house one by one. The last of the boys to leave, Bill Velasquez, is close with William and kept checking the door to see if he would show up. He has a thick beard and a goatee that drives girls crazy. Typically, he's a riot just like William. He and William are hysterically similar. They would say the same phrases or wordy random sentences at the same exact time and not be surprised when it would happen. Bill is a very touchy feely person naturally, especially with William.

They even have the same infectious laughter that would make anyone smile. Everyone except Zachariah. Z didn't like Bill when he was around William. William didn't show up at the party, though. He had to drive his sister and her friends to the beach for her birthday.

When it was just our relatives left, I handed Z the present. "Oh thanks," he said. "Who is this from?"

I took out my notebook and with a smile I neatly wrote: **William.**

Z's eyes bulged out of his head. He placed the gift back into my hands. "Uh can you put that in my room?" He scratched his head.

"Hun?" Sylvia, my stepmother, frowned. "Why don't you open it now?"

"Mhmm?" I hummed with a grin on my face.

"Murr, if you love me, and I know you do, you'd put that in my room." Sylvia locked eyes with my father who just shrugged.

I jogged upstairs and into his bedroom to place the gift on top of his bed. William was climbing in through the window dressed in a black tank top hanging low enough to see his collar bone wings tattoo and white boxer briefs.

Why do you always have to be in your underwear when you come here? I wrote.

"I guess I like to feel comfortable, you know? In my own skin." He pressed a rough chapped kiss to my forehead and rubbed it off with his thumb. "Did he open the gift?"

I held it up then shook my head.

Footsteps were heard coming up the stairs and William made a dash for the closet. Z entered the room. I sat next to Z on his unmade bed. He ripped the white box open. SpongeBob Squarepants wrapping paper was thrown recklessly everywhere on the sheets. He pulled the gifts out.

"A rainbow rhinestoned butt plug." He rolled his eyes. "God I hate that guy."

No you don't.

A wide smile slowly grew on his face as he read the black notebook. He chucked the notebook behind him and tackled me down. His fingers dug at my sides sending me into a laughing frenzy.

William bursted through the closet doors and pounced on the two of us joining in on the tickling. I couldn't breathe. I was laughing so hysterically, tears formed in my eyes.

William laid back on the bed. As I was catching my breath, William looked over at Z. "Like my gift?"

"Yeah I've been thinking about giving it to Mr. and Mr. Richardson across the street," he said.

"You're gonna use it, imbecile," William ordered holding up the butt plug to his face like a sword.

"Imbecile?" Z giggled and pushed it out of his face like a cat trying to catch a laser.

"At least give it to Sydney." William sat up. "'Z, I've been thinking about you all day," He mocked in a high pitched voice. "'This has really helped me and I think I'm ready for you now'."

I giggled and swatted Will's arm but Z's smile faded into thin air. He knocked the butt plug out of William's giant hand. He sat up, straightened out his attire, and left the room.

"Whoops." William tapped his nose and laid back against the bed with a fake worry-free smile.

Five

I think people who have faults are a lot more interesting than people who are perfect.

- Spike Lee

I've never thought I'd be in love before and I'm still not sure I'll ever be.

Don't get me wrong. It's not that I don't think love is real, it's just the idea sounds so far-fetched that it can't possibly happen to me. Like I know what love is. I've seen it physically manifested in front of my eyes. Like the time William once removed all the lice from Z's hair when they were juniors in high school. Z sat in the bathtub while William carefully removed all the bugs out of his hair with a fine tooth comb. Z, at times fidgety, kept still through it while he talked to William about his day. William was extra mad when he walked to school with Z that day only to find out he couldn't walk home with him after. He told Z he looked everywhere to find him, asking all his teachers where he was until one teacher told him that he was sent home with lice. My dad was removing the lice but then William offered to do the rest.

I'm not sure I would pull lice out of Eden's hair for her. It's not just that. It's really weird how close they are. It's like the universe wouldn't be in balance if they weren't together for at least a day. Z's always messing up somehow and William is always there to fix the problem even if it isn't purposefu.

Z had a random panic attack when he was in the shower once because he had ran out of his soap and my dad couldn't get him out. Sylvia went to the store to get that same soap but they were all sold out and it was the only open store in town at that time of night. It took about an hour before William came in the bathroom asking my dad if he had seen Z anywhere.

When he spotted him in the shower, he laughed and pulled Z out saying he got a new game for his Xbox. Z's face lit up like a child unwrapping his presents and fled into his room with William. Sometimes, William would just be calmly watching basketball on Z's tv in his bedroom laying on his stomach and Z would just casually lie on his back and promptly fall asleep. They like each other more than they like themselves. I think I know myself too well to like someone that much.

"Hi."

I stopped walking.

Avery.

Hi, is all I wrote. It's all I could think up.

"Hey, that's cute." She pointed to the notebook. I looked back up at her. Her hair was short now but still wavy and thick. It was up to her shoulders and it was dyed scarlet red. So was her matte lipstick making her lips bloom out. She was wearing a tight black leather fitting jacket, kind of like that one Bleu owned but she made it look so much better. She was wearing faded black skinny jeans and I couldn't stop staring at the sprinkled light freckles on her cheeks.

'I haven't seen you in awhile," she said quietly. Her voice was like music. She nodded with a smile as she looked me over. "You look good."

I opened my mouth but quickly put my hand over it. Shit. My heart stopped beating. I'm gonna kill myself when I get home.

Avery snorted. She placed my hand down and interlaced our cold fingers. She swung our arms side to side. "I used to do something like that when I just got my contacts. I'd try to push my glasses up when there was nothing there and I'd poke my eyes out." She laughed making me laugh.

Avery brought me back over to her house to eat ice cream sundaes we got from the Dairy Queen on the way over. Since no one was there and she forgot her keys, we ate on the dock outside her house.

"A lot has happened since I last saw you," she said swinging her feet side to side.

I heard, I wrote. I didn't want to introduce the second biggest elephant in the room. First one being me not having the ability to speak.

"Yeah. Everyone did."

Forget everyone else and just do whatever makes you happy.:)

Avery chuckled. "It was really just a distraction. When my pops died, I wanted to find a guy who'd love me as much as he did. The problem is a lot of guys don't want to love me that way. She threw her chips into the water. I watched as ducks made their way over to them hungrily.

"Maybe I haven't found the right one. The reason I

stayed away from school for so long was because sometimes I'd stand on the ledge wanting to fall as far as my heart had."

It was quiet for awhile after she said that. I began to picture her staring down from something you'd only want to walk across. "I didn't really understand people who had the abilty to kill themselves. I didn't know how to feel about them when I just didn't understand them."

I still don't.

"Don't you get it?" She bumped my shoulder with hers. "That's good. You'll never understand me. Not even if we rewinded to the day we met."

Six

What's the worst thing I've stolen? Probably little pieces of other people's lives. Where I've either wasted their time or hurt them in some way. That's the worst thing you can steal, the time of other people. You just can't get that back.

- **Chester Bennington**

"What are you thinking about?"

"Hmm?" Z dazedly looked up into Will's eyes. "What are you talking about?"

"I said what are you thinking about? You're full on staring at me. You've been doing that lately." He muttered.

Z laughed loudly. "Sorry..." He grabbed a handful of Tostitos chips and shoved it into his mouth while his other hand danced in William's chocolate curls. William glanced back at the television screen. Z gradually removed his hand from his hair and reached into Will's grey sweatpants.

"Nah man." He removed Z's hand. "Chill out."

"Why?"

"'Cause we're by the front door. Someone can walk in any minute."

"So?"

"What's the matter with you man?!"

"Will." Z smiled and propped himself up on his knees. "I had this weird dream a few nights ago."

"Great." Z kept smiling and eventually Will looked over. He sighed in annoyance. "What was the dream?"

Z shook his head. "You'll laugh at me. Or you might punch me in the face."

"Tell me."

Z smirked and whispered something in his ear. William grabbed the yellow throw pillow from behind his back and whacked him harshly repeatedly with it. Z was nearly screaming with laughter. "Stop it. Stop, I can't breathe."

"You want me to wear drag? You must be out of your fucking mind!" He sat back with a huff.

"I'm just kidding that wasn't the dream," Z insisted.

"Well I'll tell you one thing," William stated. "That definitely would have just been a dream. Sydney would have to wear that shit.

Z clenched his fists. "What did I tell you about saying her name?"

"I can say it whenever the hell I want," William said angrily.

Z watched William bore his eyes into the television screen to watch the reruns of Hey Arnold. "Please don't say it around me," Z pleaded.

"Why, so you don't feel bad for her?"

"No, so I don't feel bad for you, you big dummy."

"Man, don't worry about me I got bigger fish to fry."

"Like who?"

"What?"

"I don't know. I guess I misinterpreted what you said." Z bit his lip. "I don't even like her like that." William nodded as he kept his focus on watching the television screen. "Will?" He played with a dark brown lengthy curl.

William ignored him.

Z laughed. "Bigger fish to fry." He put Will's head against his chin and rubbed his arm. I smiled down at the scene from the railing trying not to come off as creepy. "Wanna know what I actually dreamed about?" Z asked.

"What?"

"Sydney and I got married with two kids."

"Weird."

"Yeah and then you died. That's it."

"That's it?"

"I was crying a lot. I cried a lot and then I woke up."

William nodded.

"Anyway," Z said trying to keep a straight face. "I hope you don't die." William began cackling.

-

I always liked Avery but for the longest time I had no idea I liked her that way. I can recall being taken aback that one time she passed by my uncle's car on the highway with this 20-something year old guy with a bushy beard. I was sitting in the car with my uncle and she was standing up through the sunroof looking radiant against the wind. She was standing up reading a book while her hair was whipping back with the breeze. I remember watching up at her in awe while my uncle went off about millennials and the stupidity that comes with them. Avery peered down at me and waved with the most impressive smile. But even then, I didn't know I was gay.

A building, a few blocks from my street that my dad rented out for the talent company he's been working for, is being used as a dance studio. I come in here to think sometimes or just to breathe. I love the solitude. I practice talking in front of the mirrors in the last room at the end of the hall but nothing ever works. I even tried singing but my words only fell into a hum.

No one is here around the time I come in except the janitor occasionally if he comes in at 6-7. He cleans at 8 and leaves the doors open sometimes. He's really lazy like me.

As I was writing in my notebook, a thump came in from down the hall. I figured it was the janitor until the "janitor" said 'Holy Shit! That hurt'.

I rose from the smooth wooden floor and dashed out into the hall. It was empty. I followed where the rustling was coming from and peaked into a room where a familiar redhead laid sprawled on the wooden floor. I quickly hid behind the wall. Avery jumped up off the ground and backed up to the wall inside the studio.

Then I watched her dance in the mirror.

She spun in circles like a crimson silk sheet being thrown slowly across a bed. She did random dance moves in a jerky fashion with her arms. She paused and looked at herself before rupturing into chuckles. Avery stared down at her feet and placed her hands up against the mirror. "Spread 'em."

I bit the inside of my cheek attempting not to laugh.

Avery quickly turned around dramatically against the mirror. "No officer please no...no...n-," she slid down the mirror and once she was sitting on the floor, she closed her eyes and stuck her tongue out pretending to be dead. She turned around and did a handstand against the mirror. It lasted for about 10 seconds before she lightly dropped to her head, rolled on to her back and looked at herself. She stared at herself woebegone before she laughed at her face in the mirror.

She placed her green fedora, with a light and dark brown striped feather hanging out on the side of it, over her face and groaned aggressively.

Avery stood up and went over and carefully pressed her soft pink lips up against the mirror fogging it up. She looked at the mirror with desperation before she mouthed my name.

I've been admiring her for months now even before she was enrolled back into the high school.

I caught Avery at Dave and Busters where she was riding a fake motorcycle with some guy with jet black hair in a ponytail and sleeve tattoos. Her head tossed back in laughter. I didn't mean to stare for so long from where I was standing, but I did.

Avery watched the guy get off the motorcycle and when it was her turn to get off, she spotted me.

"Mercury!" She waved. I waved still mesmerized. "I was just about to go and get something to eat. Wanna come?"

We decided on Mary's diner. I just prayed Eden wouldn't see us here because this would be the time of her shift.

"I love this place. It's cozy." She shrugged her white bubble coat off before pausing to look up at me. "You know what?" Avery stood up and sat down right next to me with a warm smile.

I tried my best not to blush. My heart jumped out of my chest and onto the wooden table when I saw Eden standing in front of us.

"Hi, my name is Eden. I'll be your server for today.

What would you like to order?" She avoided eye contact with me looking straight at Avery.

"Hi." Avery's eyes roamed the menu. "Um can I have a cheeseburger with fries? No pickles please. And a big strawberry shake so we can share. With lots of whipped cream."

"Alright." She wrote the order down and then stared at me with a neutral expression. "For you?"

Avery threw her arm around me protectively. "My friend'll have the same thing."

I nodded pleased. Something about Avery made me feel like I shouldn't be afraid of anything. Like she was a pain reliever. I couldn't feel anything but completely numb.

"Alright I'll be right back." Eden harshly collected the menus and left. Avery began playing with my feet under the table as she poked her pink tongue out in concentration. "She's from our school isn't she?"

Kicking back, I nodded.

"She's kind of cute."

I kicked her hard.

"Ow!" She jumped. I stuck my tongue out at her. "What was that for, pequena mierda?" She laughed. "You like her or something?"

I furrowed my eyebrows and shook my head.

"Here." Eden slammed the shake down on the table harshly, some of the whip cream flew away onto the table. "Someone will be here with your food shortly. Enjoy!" Then she left.

"What the hell was that about?"

I just shrugged and took a sip of our shake.

Seven

To succeed, jump as quickly at opportunities as you do at conclusions.

• Benjamin Franklin

I strolled up to Eden smiling. She was on her fuchsia bike outside her house texting someone. I tapped her on the shoulder and she turned around to face me.

"I don't like your girlfriend," she said not looking up. "Or your friend. I don't know. I just don't. You should know I don't because she's all-"

My face felt like it was melting into the Earth's core. Avery is the only thing I can think about to calm myself down.

"God." Eden laughed and rubbed her light brown cheeks. "Speaking to you is really something because whatever I say in my head I immediately say it out loud. God it's like I'm talking to myself. Like I'm talking to noth..." She jerked her frightened gaze up at me. I didn't know what to do with my hands so I tried walking away but all I could do was turn my back to her. Every step I took made me feel as if I were on a treadmill.

"I didn't mean that. I'm just worried about you. Bye."

She threw her bike on the ground and ran inside her home. Disappointedly, I stared down at my feet that seemed to be glued to the pavement, truly feeling sorry for myself for the first time in a while.

I woke up in a cold sweat. I was breathing heavily. It was just a nightmare. I opened my window to be hit by the cool refreshing midnight air. Sliding out under my window, I pressed my feet onto the damp roof. There were still puddles left over from last night's heavy rain. I lifted Eden's already opened window and stepped into her room quietly. Eden was fast asleep giving out tiny snores while drool made its way to her white pillow case. She was in nothing but her underwear with one leg under the comforter and one leg above it. The floor outside the door creaked and immediately, I scurried into the closet.

Bleu entered the room and quietly perched on the edge of Eden's bed. She pulled down the beaded switch of the beige bedside lamp. In her hand was a tube of Neosporin, a damp cloth, and a few band aids. Squinting, she placed them all on the nightstand. Bleu grabbed Eden's arm.

I bit back a scream. Her entire arm was covered in fine lined raised scars and red cuts. Bleu reached for the soaking wet yellow cloth and put it against Eden's arm. Eden slowly began to wake up. She sat up startled when she realized it was Bleu in front of her. "Bleu what are you doing?"

Bleu didn't say anything. She finished gently putting Neosporin along the cuts. Eden's eyes started closing again as if they were magnets. Bleu placed the band aids over her marks.

"Bleu the band aids are too noticeable," she whispered.

"You can take them off in the morning, alright?"

Eden complied and instantly fell back asleep. Bleu leaned down to kiss her forehead. She rose from the pink polka dotted sheet and turned the light back off.

"Got it." Avery stepped down from the concrete step outside of the tattoo shop. She was wearing a red cropped tank top with high waisted shorts and her lustrous red lipstick again. Her hair was in a red bun with strands loosely falling on the sides.

Got what? I wrote. I looked over at the women printed in several tattoos with a blonde low buzz cut staring at the two of us walk away with a smile.

"Nothing," she said with a grin. "Let's go."

I tried to peek into the brown paper bag. She put it in her other hand. "Nosy nosy."

Going to a party, tonight? I asked.

"No?"

Any plans?

"Why?"

Just curious.

"I'm not having sex tonight I'm staying in. Happy?"

What are you gonna do?

"Think about someone."

Who?

"I don't know, okay? It varies."

Are you mad at me?

"What?" She stopped walking. I shrugged. "Why would I be mad at you? You haven't done anything wrong." She stepped closer to me narrowing her eyes. "Are you used to feeling that way?"

43

I looked behind us at the woman. I wrote, ***Are you a mind reader?***

"Shit." She put her dainty hands on her hips. Her red tinted heart shaped sunglasses slid down to the bridge of her nose. She looked up at me with a sympathetic facial expression. "You don't tell people about what happened. Do you?"

I avoided her gaze. She wasn't going to continue walking until I responded so I just shook my head.

Avery puffed out her cheeks and released a breath of air. She pushed her sunglasses up and wrapped her arm around my shoulders. We started our steady stride again in silence. "I don't get you sometimes. And no I'm not a mind reader I've just dealt with the same shit. It's common."

-

Our school has a fundraiser once a year every October at the nearby boardwalk to raise money for the school, programs/clubs and sports teams. The place is buzzing with teenagers. Everyone around, who attended the high school, still goes there which is why I wasn't surprised to see my brother and his girlfriend delving into their fluffy pink cotton candy. Sydney was calmly feeding the airy food into his mouth with a smile.

I dug my sweaty palms into my sea blue jacket pockets. I'm not saying I only came to see Avery but if I said I didn't, I would be lying. I spotted Bleu and her boyfriend Stuart behind the kissing booth. Bleu was on the stool and her blonde hair was curlier than normal.

Zachariah came up behind me and rubbed my back. "What time did you get here?"

I opened my notebook and scribbled the words ***just now.***

"Hey," William came up to Sydney, Z, and I with a

girl who had two Afro puffs in her hair. She was as tall as William with a luminescent smile and gold eyeshadow. "This is Drea. Drea, this is Mercury." He playfully pulled my ear lobe. "She's really nice and this is Z."

"Oh so you're Z?" Drea said. "Heard a lot about you."

"I hope that's not a bad thing," Z chuckled.

Drea smiled politely. She looked over at William trying not to laugh as her cherry lips grew into a smile.

"Um," Z spoke absentmindedly. "This is Sydney."

"Hi." Drea shook hands with her.

"Alright c'mon the line is getting longer." William pulled her hand. "See you, Z."

"Nice to meet you guys." Drea raced down the boardwalk with William.

Z scratched his blond hair clearly confused about what just happened.

"C'mon I saw Stacey." Sydney happily linked their arms and headed over to two preppy girls and one bored guy standing by the Ferris wheel.

Eden walked up to me dressed in a backwards orange cap and a Seaworld t-shirt with a giant red x drawn over it. "Hey."

Hi, I wrote.

"You didn't have to write that." I shrugged. "I saw William. And Z."

Will's just mad. Both of them are.

"I came here with Bleu. She wanted me to meet some of her friends but I left. She invited me to this party a couple weekends ago and I went. It wasn't all that. I would've brought you but you said you hate parties so."

The scene was replaying in my mind of Bleu helping

Eden last night. I struggled to not look at Eden's sleeved arms. She needs a friend. She needs someone to talk to.

Why? They could be okay.

"They're all the same." She looked around. "All of them look the same. All of them act the same."

Bleu kissed a tall boy with ginger hair and accepted the five dollars. Stuart stared him down until he left.

I don't like your sister too much, I wrote. But she's good for you, I wanted to say. She's doing what's best for you.

Eden read it and laughed. "I wouldn't expect anyone in their right mind to." Eden was probably thinking about yesterday, too.

I clutched my pencil. ***I'm sorry***. For everything. I told myself to write that in later.

"Don't be," she said unbothered. "She's a bitch."

Avery jumped in front of me. "Boo!"

I was unfazed by it but Eden jumped out of her skin.

"Well I got one of you." Avery softly gazed over at me and bumped our shoulders with a smile. "Sup."

I blushed instantly.

"I remember you." She pointed at Eden.

"It's a small town," she said looking past her. "Good thing you did."

Avery scratched behind her ear. She appeared downhearted as she looked back at me. "Uh I was gonna head over to the bottle ring toss." She jerked her thumb behind her. "They're promoting Dick's sporting goods." A smile grew on her face as she spoke. "So the prizes are these teddy bears that say "I love Dick's!" It's pretty funny."

I snorted.

She rubbed her fuzzy grey gloved hands together and tucked them under her arms. "You guys wanna come?"

"You guys can go," Eden insisted. "I was gonna get an ice cream."

Avery nodded. I watched Eden awkwardly leave. "Wow she really doesn't like me."

I don't know why she's acting like that.

"Shit happens. I promise this is the last thing I do before I head home and I really want that bear." Avery turned around and stopped in her tracks when she spotted Bleu and Stuart. "Never mind we should stay back here."

It's fine.

Avery bit her lip. She wrapped an arm around my shoulder and walked with me to the bottle ring toss station with my head against hers. Avery stopped and stared at Bleu's kissing booth. "Jesus H."

Quincy was leaning against the counter of the booth with a smile. "Sup."

"No," Bleu said instantaneously.

"What? Isn't this for a charity? What's the cause?"

"Our soccer team."

"Oh okay," Quincy said. "That's pretty good."

"No way."

"Oh come on." She smiled with her hands on the booth. "5 seconds isn't that the limit?" Quincy asked Stuart.

"Sure is," he said holding back a laugh.

Quincy smiled over at Bleu. "Well?"

"No. No way I'm not doing it."

"C'mon it's good money," Stuart said with his palm over his mouth.

I watched as Quincy looked back at her girlfriend,

whose name I found out was Lily. She was snarling at Bleu and talking to a flamboyant guy in bright sparkly pink pants listening to her inaudible commentary.

"Fine if it'll get you to leave," Bleu said quickly while staring at Lily, too.

"Really?"

Her eyes flickered to Quincy like a dancing candle flame. Bleu's nostrils were flared as she was staring at the counter of the booth. Quincy kept vengefully staring at her eyes. "Alright let's do it." Bleu rolled her eyes but closed them anyway. Quincy hesitantly looked back again with a smug smile. Lily scowled and walked off with the colorful guy to the Ferris wheel.

Quincy looked back at Bleu and leaned in to gently press her full brownish pink lips against Bleu's. Bleu's expression gradually softened like a child's after hours of nonstop crying.

It took me a minute to realize that my rivaling co-captains were kissing right in front of me. Bleu, the girl that once purposefully tripped Quincy as she was about to make a team goal and Quincy the girl who smeared a concoction of deodorant and Gatorade onto Bleu's uniform shorts "by accident". Stuart's controlled hysteria wavered once he saw Bleu's anger cease. After what I counted to be about five seconds, Quincy moved away slowly but Bleu kept her lips attached.

"Time, Bleu," Stuart muttered confused.

Bleu popped off. "Oh." Her entire face flushed scarlet. What she was thinking was written all over her face in ink and she knew it. She rubbed at her cheeks to smudge the writing in.

Quincy stared at her lips and then up at her light blue

eyes before frowning. She handed the money to Stuart and walked past us.

"Holy shit," Avery said.

"Shut up." Quincy said harshly. She took off in the direction Lily went off in.

-

The bell over the door rang when I entered the restaurant. I scanned the aisles for her and saw a familiar head of curly ginger hair staring out the window. I sat down in the red plastic covered booth and slid in front of Eden but she just kept her stagnant gaze out the window.

You're not gonna let me have friends are you. I stared at what I wrote for a minute deciding whether or not I should show this to her. Reluctantly, I tapped the table to get her attention. Eden read out of my notebook. She rolled her eyes. "I just don't like her."

Why?

"Because she sleeps with everybody. She can do whatever the hell she wants and still be able to sleep at night."

Who cares if she sleeps around? It's her body.

Eden gave a bittersweet smile. "I'm sure you don't care, Mercury. You're always so interested in people who stick out of a crowd." I felt like how I usually feel after running along the track for 20 minutes: tired. Hopeless at the idea of running again. Out of energy. I put my pen and notepad away and stared at the booth across from me waiting to see if she'd speak to me again. She didn't. I released one of those dramatic sighs Z usually let's out when he doesn't get what he wants. I stood up and left the restaurant.

-

By the time Z got home, after dropping off Sydney

at her home, it was past 10 PM. My dad and I were on the couch watching a movie with his wife, Sylvia. Sylvia is nearly ten years younger than my father. At first I was kind of mad at my dad about it but then I started to realize how similar Sylvia and I are. We're awkward, unable to know what to say in awkward situations and we both still have so much energy. She's Samoan and always wears a Samoan Sei (a hair flower). Every day it's a different color for a different emotion. Her emotions range from euphoric to content. That still drives me up the wall. When Z busted through the door, he shut it closed and roughy scratched his blond hair. His cheeks were in a hot blush from the cold. He glanced over at me and paused. He was angry. His icy glare penetrated my eyes. I began to look away as soon as I started feeling uncomfortable but it was too late.

"Whatever the fuck you think is going on, isn't going on! I mean it. Nothing. He's a worthless faggot. He's a complete idiot and he's nothing but a pathetic sorry son of a bitch-" He inhaled sharply. "Who gets off on making people's lives worse than his own, okay!?" I looked at my dad who was staring up at Z, trying to hear him out. "I don't want you around that freak anymore." Z walked upstairs and slammed his door closed. My dad was wearing a concerned expression on his face. He scooted closer to me.

"Tell me what that was about."

I froze. My dad doesn't know about the two of them. What am I supposed to say?

"Now."

I wrote, ***Will just made him feel small and he doesn't know why.***

To my surprise, my dad started snickering, he looked

at a shaken up Sylvia and then back at me. "They used to have heated arguments like that ever since you were a baby. They'll work it out."

"Hey, kid." Will leaned against the banister by the porch steps I was perched on.

Not supposed to talk to you.

"Oh yeah?" William read.

Why'd Drea laugh at Z?

"I told her he used to have long brown hair that made him look like Shaggy from Scooby Doo."

I giggled. ***He's really mad at you.***

William scoffed, waving me off. "He's always mad at me."

For real this time.

William stares down at what I wrote. He blinked a few times before shrugging and looking at something in the distance. Almost as if on cue, Z walked past the two of us and over to the drive way to get in his car. "I should give him some space?" William asked. "It's that bad?"

I nodded. William took a seat next to me. He spoke quietly with a straight serious expression molded onto his face while looking down at his hands. "I shouldn't have brought the girl."

She's pretty, I offered.

"Oh yeah she should be. She's my cousin."

I laughed boisterously and instantly covered my mouth.

Z jerked his head up over at us for a split second before fumbling with his keys again. William snickered tickling my side. "I'm gonna give him a few days."

Evil.

"I know."

Avery approached the two of us with her golden retriever. She was wearing a grey plaid flannel and a backwards Nike cap. "Hey."

The large dog leaped on to me and licked at my face.

"Hey," William said.

"Hi, Will. How've you been?"

"Good. You?"

"Fine." Avery tried pulling the dog back.

"How's school?"

I laughed when the dog started licking my ear.

"Pretty good actually," Avery answered. "College?"

"Better than ever."

"Yeah. I didn't mean to interrupt. Good to see you." She waved and winked at me. "See you around, Mercury."

I waved back and then to the golden retriever that whimpered when he was pulled away from me.

"Now *she* grew up nicely."

I kicked him roughly.

"Ow! Damn, girl."

I jogged back into the house feeling pleased with myself.

Eight

I'm a human being and I fall in love and sometimes I don't have control of every situation.

- Beyoncé Knowles-Carter

How do you ask someone out?

Quincy invited me over because we never actually hung out outside of school. We were lounging in her bedroom. The walls were painted peach and she had a tiny TV set up on her dresser.

"It depends on the person really. Why? You tryna ask me out?" She was sipping the passion fruit juice she offered me that I politely declined from a large pink Hello Kitty cup. She was wearing a red Reebok hoodie and SpongeBob pajama pants as she sat beside me on her full sized bed. I peered up at her with a grin and shook my head boldly. I was getting chilly from the air conditioner blowing cold air from the window where it was mounted.

"Who you wanna ask out?"

You'll laugh at me.

"Not if you tell me not, too."

Do not laugh.

"Deal." She smiled. "Now spill."

I grabbed my pencil trying to roll off the comforter and sat up from lying on my belly. *Avery.* Then it hit me. Oh my god, I just came out. I tried not to let it show that I was momentarily losing my shit. At that moment, I wasn't sure what I was more surprised about: my ability to write it out so quickly or the fact that for the first ten seconds I didn't think it mattered. Quincy didn't seem too surprised either. She just rubbed her chin and said, "Hmm interesting."

Why?

"All she does is sleep with guys. She's nice, though."

Saying she'll let me down easy?

"No come on that's not what I meant. Just be honest. She loves honesty."

I've been practicing talking.

Quincy looked at me with an impressed grin. "Oh yeah?"

Yeah.

"How's that going?"

Not good, I wanted to write. I shrugged instead.

"You've been hanging out with her a lot lately?" I nodded. Maybe it'll work. "Who knows?"

I flicked her ear. *Don't tell any of your friends.* She had so many friends.

"I ain't like that. I'll tell you a secret if that'll make you happy."

Do tell.

Quincy looked over at the door for precaution and then back down at me. "If my dad comes up in here and he hears what I say, I'm gonna hurt you." I smiled. "Okay so you know Lily right?"

I nodded.

"She...put her mouth on me."

Okay? And?

"Not like a kiss okay like..." She bit her tongue. "I'm talkin' 'bout...on me."

I made sure to display the amount of disgust I had. "Ugh."

"Oh now you can speak? That's what lesbians do I just never had someone do it to me." She put her palms against her chest. "And what do you mean by 'ugh'. I'm not dry."

I covered my ears.

Quincy shook her head. "You're so naive. It's not disgusting if you actually like the person."

You really like her? I asked.

"She's not June, but yeah."

You have a thing for June?

"Everyone knows. Even Bleu knows." Bleu, Bleu, Bleu.

Bleu's into you.

"Now that's 'ugh' right there. She still hasn't apologized to me with her racist ugly thin lipped pasty lookin' ass."

I think she's into her, too.

-

"Sweetie can I borrow your laptop," Sylvia asked me when I got home at midnight. I nodded and pointed upstairs. "Okay great, thanks. Mine just stopped working all of a sudden. I made seafood paella. It's on the stove." I smelt it the minute I walked in. I smiled so that she could smile back before heading up the stairs. I grabbed a bottle from the fridge. When I pulled my phone out of my pocket I had three missed calls from Avery. As soon as I tried to unlock my phone, it shut off due to low battery. My charger was in my room so I headed upstairs.

Sylvia was at my desk opening the laptop. Suddenly moaning and curse words were flying around the room like wild moths. On the screen were two topless girls laying on each other.

Sylvia screamed in a fashion that I realized would be amusing if this whole event wasn't happening to me. I quickly snatched the laptop from her and exited out.

"I'm so sorry," she said. Sylvia was waving her hands around and rested them over her eyes. Everything was exaggerated in the moment. I wiped my forehead and put the laptop back down before leaving the room.

I made the mistake of telling Quincy what happened the next day. She was laughing hysterically. I roughly punched her in the arm. I was consumed with embarrassment that was coalescing with anger.

"How are you gonna let yourself get caught like that? You practically gave her the evidence."

I hope she doesn't tell my dad, I quickly wrote. I sucked my teeth. I didn't even think about that.

"It doesn't matter, okay? It doesn't matter. It's almost 2018."

You haven't told anyone I'm gay right?

"No! Please. Don't you trust me?" Quincy looked out my window. "You really shouldn't have invited me over. She probably thinks we're dating now."

My eyes widened. I was not thinking today.

Quincy looked back at me. "Doesn't Eden know you're gay?"

I don't know.

She fixed her eyes from her notebook to the window again. "Is that Bleu with your brother?"

I looked out the window. Bleu was sitting cross legged in front of Z while Z was picking at the grass with his hands. Bleu was radiating a toothy smile while Z was babbling about something. This was one of the things that made me genuinely smile. A genuine smile is a smile you can't control. Natural happenstances aren't always beautiful but just satisfying enough to your eyes to make it "beautiful", too. Society has taught us to not label that beauty but that's what beauty really is.

"She likes him?"

Nah, they're like best friends. But I didn't tell her that.

"I think she does." Quincy was staring at the beauty.

Bleu's into you, I wrote again.

"Quit saying that." She laughed. Her gaze on Bleu didn't waver.

She talks to him about stuff. I tapped her shoulder to show her what I wrote.

"What stuff?"

I thought about how I would phrase that. ***Things Will makes fun of him for because it sounds too soft.***

"Bleu talks to him about that stuff?"

I nodded.

"Since when is she nice?"

She's always nice to Z.

Avery invited me to the beach. She lived by the shore so we weren't far from her home. She had a bottle of Merlot planted in the sand. We were both just staring out at the living water crash against each other. Each wave fought each other like they were in combat. Avery was slightly tipsy.

"I've been thinking about you. And when I say 'been' I mean for a hell of a long time I've been thinking about you. And-" She laughed. "I know you've been thinking about me now because everyone's thinking about me like that now. But I thought of you, even during the moments you didn't ever think to think of me." She snorted and fell back into the sand laughing.

That's a lot of thinking.

"Yeah." She smiled up at the sky. "It is." She paused for a moment but then she said. "Remember in 8th grade we were running to the bus and you slipped on the ice then I slipped on the ice?"

I tried to forget. One of the most embarrassing moments of my life. I grinned and nodded.

Avery tried not to smile. "I didn't slip on the ice.".

My smile faded.

"I didn't want you to feel embarrassed and I ended up cutting my lip open and I chipped some of my tooth. Right here." She pointed to her tooth a little lower than the others. I went to grab my notebook from the sand.

"I went on the bus because you seemed like you were in the moment and you were smiling. I had these pocket tissues in my bag and I used them all up by the time we got to school." The apples of Avery's cheeks turned rosy pink. "I went to the nurse the second I got off the bus and went back home. I can't believe I'm saying this much shit out loud!" She screamed out loud. "The wine, Mercury, it's going to my head." She laid back down in the sand. I ran my fingers along her stomach. "I don't need anything from you, Mercury." She said staring at the sky again. I opened my notebook but Avery clamped her hand over it. I looked up at her but Avery was staring at me with a gaze I couldn't find the emotion to.

She sat up, took the notebook, and read from it before I had a chance to oppose. "Everything you've said for the past few months are on these pages?" She flipped the page and stared at a paragraph. "Were you arguing with someone here?" I read the page: "***You're always driving them away. Soon enough you won't be able to hold onto your own shit.***" I gently retrieved the book and closed it.

"I'm sorry. I shouldn't have pried. I'm an idiot."

I shook my head. I saw Avery from the corner of my eye.

Avery was looking at me worriedly. I laughed from the dramatic silliness of it all and stared at my hands dangling off my knees. I listened to the ocean some more. She handed me the wine bottle. I shook my head.

"Yes." She set it next to me. "Just for today."

I don't know.

"Please. For me."

I took a sip.

Half an hour rolled by at 50 miles per hour. I was gone. I was dizzy. I was happy. I didn't feel anything. I still felt sorry for myself but it wasn't myself. I felt sorry for Mercury as if Mercury wasn't me.

"Do you think love will become obsolete?" Avery asked. I tried to steady myself as I gripped Avery who appeared hazy. We walked up a never ending grassy hill.

I saw the purple clouds behind it. We were getting higher and higher "I think love is evil and it's just gonna outlive us all." I laughed because she was serious. "Maybe it already... has." I fell to the floor making Avery fall, too. She began cracking up.

I laid on my back and stared at the purple sky.

Everything was purple.

"C'mon." She was still laughing. She tugged at my orange bomber jacket sleeve. "C'mon."

I shook my head.

Avery climbed on top of me and randomly took her shirt off revealing a black lace bra. She laid back against my propped up legs.

I traced along her skin. All the freckles on her stomach making her shiver. "I really want you but I'm never gonna tell you. You'll never find out." She fell back into the grass when my legs began to wobble. "Keep it." She put her oversized white t-shirt in my face. "I'm too drunk."

It smelled like strawberries so I didn't take it off.

Nine

There is a light at the end of the tunnel... hopefully it's not a freight train!

- **Mariah Carey**

A bell chimed a couple times. I looked up and saw Bleu rolling up to me on a green old fashioned cruiser bicycle. "You think I like her don't you?" She asked circling me.

I dizzily stared at her. I rotated in a circle to follow where she went. Her hair was frizzy and she had dark circles under her eyes.

"Because of the kiss you think I like her?" She was grinning playfully but you can tell she was pissed. "And you told her didn't you because I know you and that other girl were her only friends who saw us kiss."

That's not why I think you like her.

"Why then?" She asked. She stopped her bike and folded her arms across her chest. She appeared as though she were a god looking down at me from her place in the heavens as I surrendered to her.

Did you know I was there?

"When?"

When you kissed her in the booth. Did you know anyone was there? Hear anyone?

Bleu read it over and looked up at me. "No. It was weird. How did you know that happened?" She sat up straighter.

I heard that happens sometimes, I wrote honestly.

You can talk to me if you want.

Bleu biked off hastily.

-

My phone kept going off at the dinner table. It was the only noise being made at the table other than the clinking of forks and knives against the porcelain plates.

I made an attempt to discreetly check it but the minute I saw what was on my phone I choose ked on my macaroni salad. Obscene nude pictures of Avery were in my messages.

"Mercury," my father scolded. "I told you no phones at the dinner table." I nodded but the phone went off again once I put it down. I put it on vibrate.

"Don't look at it," my dad said eyeing me.

I nodded.

"Maria's having a party at her house on Satur-" The phone buzzed. "-day," Sylvia finished. She cleared her throat. "All the neighbors are invited."

"That's nice of her," my dad said.

My phone vibrated twice.

"We don't have to bring anything do we?" My dad asked.

"You really want to go?"

"Yeah, c'mon," he said with hesitancy in his voice. "It'd be fun." The phone went off again. "Mercury, can you tell whoever that is to stop please."

I frustratedly grabbed my phone off the table. My phone was filled with obscene photos from Avery and texts from

Eden. I sent the same text to both of them: *Cut it out. I'm eating dinner with my family.* Z peeked down at my phone but I hid it just in time.

Well hurry up I'm in your room, Eden texted back sending a picture of herself on my bed. Avery was the next one to text me. *We really need to talk:)*

Sylvia, fortunately, didn't even have the guts to look at me during dinner. At least I think she didn't. I didn't have the balls either. Imagine falling in love with a man who seems like the perfect guy for you but then you get married and have to be a stepmother to a bipolar man and his mute gay sister. I've never acknowledged Sylvia and my dad's relationship as one based on love but I guess their relationship could be used as an example of it. So far, love, to me, has been defined as having a boost of adrenaline for dealing with other people's baggage and bullshit.

After dinner, I headed into my room and over to Eden on my bed who was eating mint chocolate chip ice cream.

"Want some?"

I nodded. I tried reaching for it but she chose to feed it to me with a spoon. I laughed.

"Good?" She asked. I felt like a baby. I nodded regardless.

"Anyway, I know you're like in love with Avery."

I didn't panic. From the passive aggressive look on her face, I could tell she was bluffing.

"When Avery says hi to you, this is you." Eden rolled her eyes back into her head. "Oh my god oh my god yes yes ahhhh." She calmly ate her ice cream again. She was so amusing. "I know you love her."

You don't know what love is, I wrote.

"Excuse me?" Eden asked as if it was a scandalous remark.

I raised one eyebrow in my defense.

"What is it then?" She asked.

Worship.

"Yeah? Well you worship Avery. You probably kiss the ground she walks on."

I smirked and wrote, **You're just jealous we're getting along so well**.

Eden stared at the paper. She abruptly ripped it out of the notebook and teared it up in front of my face before standing up and collecting her things. I stood up in front of her with a smile blocking her from leaving. Eden didn't look up and stared at the ground gripping her bag. "Move." She said unable to keep a straight face.

I pushed her back onto the bed and laid beside her. We both stared up at the ceiling. Mine was spinning.

She spoke quietly. "I started praying."

I paused. I held my breath.

"So that you can talk again." She gulped. I forgot how to. Does she even remember my voice? That thought made me open my mouth but Eden instantly covered it. "Oh stop pretending like you're going to say something when you're not." Her voice cracked. "I don't like it when you do that anymore." She pushed off of me and headed out the window to her room.

I bit my pillow and screamed into it.

-

The next day I was about to leave my bedroom to see Avery when Z suddenly stormed in and roughly put his hand around my throat throwing me against the wall. "Why were you laughing at me?" He asked through gritted teeth. I stared at myself in the mirror. Z was gripping me so tightly, my legs dangled low above the ground. I tried getting out of his strong hold but I couldn't breathe. "Murr, why were you laughing at me?! You know..." he tightened his grip breathing heavily. "I don't like people laughing at me." I tried making a sound but it came out incomprehensible.

"Tell me!" He shouted. My face was turning a deep shade of purple. I'm gonna die, I thought to myself. I was already accepting it. My brother's gonna kill me. The room was beginning to be encased by darkness.

"Hey!" William burst into the room. "Drop her now."

Z was still glaring at me with cold lifeless eyes.

William inched closer to us. "I said drop her. Now."

Z, still breathing heavily, dropped me to the floor. I broke into an uneasy loud coughing fit. There was a pale hand print around my blood red tinted neck.

"Close your eyes," William told Z.

Z turned around angrily. "I don't have to listen to you!"

"Hey!" William pointed a finger in his face. "Close your eyes." He gently covered his hand over Z's eyes. When he removed them Z's eyes were closed shut. William set him down on my mattress.

Z started to ugly cry like a heartbroken child. "You were laughing at me, Mercury was laughing at me and Drea was laughing at me." He shook his head and covered his ears. "Everyone was laughing at me."

I was so overcome with anxiety. I placed a hand over my mouth and sprinted into the bathroom. After lifting the seat up, I threw up violently in the toilet watching everything that has happened recently get released into the porcelain bowl.

"Mercury?!" I heard William faintly call out from my room. "Z, count back from 200 until I tell you to stop."

"200, 199, 198, 197..."

"Hey." A large hand rubbed my back. I stifled a cry.

"I know," William handed me toilet paper. I leaned back against the wall and weakly smiled at him. William smiled, too. "Feeling better?"

I threw up again, some of it getting on my Hawaiian shirt. I was thinking about Eden. I felt so bad for her. I felt worse for her than I did for myself.

"Woah alright take that shirt off. I'm gonna get you another one." William ran out of the bathroom. I pitied William, too, for loving Z and I so hard. I rubbed my temples and took my shirt off. The cool air hit my bare chest.

"Can I stop now?" Z asked.

"No, you can't." Will came back. He had a large St. Lucia t-shirt in his hand. Probably from Z's room that he had left there, I thought. "Come here Mercury." He turned the sink on. I automatically washed my mouth out and grabbed the toothbrush from William.

"Don't brush too far back or you'll throw up again." He flushed the toilet and put the shirt on the counter before leaving the bathroom. I couldn't wear this to Avery's.

"Is she okay?" I heard Z ask.

"Don't put your hands on a girl ever again." I stared at myself in the mirror. This time, not on the verge of death. "Don't ever do it again. Or I will hurt you so bad, man. I mean it."

"I won't do it again!"

"Why are you yelling at me?" I heard Will ask softly.

"Because I get it."

I bit my lip trying not to break into another sob. William was quiet before he said. "Drea isn't my girlfriend. She's my cousin. And I'm sorry I laughed at you. I was joking around about your old hair."

Then Z was quiet. "Why didn't you just tell me?"

"I don't know," William choked out.

"You've been a real jerk lately," Z said. Then he laughed so he could lighten the mood. Like putting lol after a text message. William stayed silent. I came back into the room and sat on the far edge of the bed. William was kneeling in front of Z with his head in his lap. After a minute, Z hugged me. "I'm sorry, Murr."

I started to bawl and hugged him back as tight as I could.

"I'm sorry, too," William said.

-

Avery was walking her golden retriever again. I bravely stood in her way. I was wearing a Golden State Warriors Basketball Jersey because it was the only shirt I had left that wasn't in my laundry. The muscles in my arms that I've always been self conscious about, rather than proud of, were prominent. Avery was gawking so I hid them behind my back. I wore my lucky eyebrow ring. I cleared my throat. I pretended that she was the mirror in the dance studio. A smeared dirty mirror. A crimson silk sheet slowly fell over the mirror.

"I was waiting for you," she started. "Why didn't-"

"Go out with me," a deep voice said. YES. YES YES YES. It was me.

Avery's face lit up like Christmas lights. She shook my shoulders baffled with her jaw melting slowly to the floor. "Yeah, okay."

"And sit with me at lunch tomorrow. My dad's making snickerdoodles with my brother tonight and I'm gonna bring some in tomorrow so you can eat them." YES YES. I missed rambling.

She nodded fervently. "Okay."

I nodded. "Okay. Bye."

"Bye. I like your piercing."

"Thank you. I like your face."

"I like yours, too."

I nodded. "I have to go some place now." I lied. There's was nowhere I had to go. No one was expecting me anywhere.

"Bye, Mercury."

I blinked and frowned at myself once I turned to leave. When I turned around to see her, she was jumping up and down. She started spinning in circles like a lunatic. A loony toon with birds and swirls flying over her head. I let out a contented sigh.

The next day she sat down next to me. Eden poking at her salad, looked down at her plate like it was the most interesting thing in the world.

"Hello," Avery said. She was wearing a black crop top with the words Cry Baby bedazzled on it short enough to see her entire belly. "Do you have my cookies?"

Graham, some weird guy I listen to sometimes, jerked his head up. I handed the golden brown snickerdoodles to her.

"Thank you." She put her hand on my thigh as she ate her cookies.

Meanwhile, Quincy was licentiously making out with Lily at the end of our lunch table.

Avery whispered in my ear. "I have never gone out with a girl before. Are we supposed to be doing that?" I snorted.

"Dykes," Bleu said under her breath. She walked past

Quincy and Lily when she said it. She said it as loud as she could, too.

Quincy broke away and turned around. "What did you just call me?"

"I didn't say anything. Did you hear me say something?"

"I didn't hear anything," Cassidy said. Her mouth was like a horse's when she chewed her gum. She smiled devilishly.

"Apologize," Quincy said. Her eyes didn't waver from Bleu's.

Bleu smirked. "For what?"

"For calling us dykes. Apologize now."

"No I'm not apologizing under scrutiny that's based off of a delusion."

I looked at Eden. She just started picking her salad once more. Quincy pointed at the three of them. "I don't care if it was Cassidick, Ratchet Rachel or you, basic Bitchy Bleu. I want...an apology...now."

Bleu pretended to ponder it for a minute. "No." She raised her eyebrows with a bold smile.

Eden tensed up from across the table. Quincy's eyes softened. Her face was smug. "You know what?" She raised her hands up. "It's cool. If it was you, and I know it was you, I know you didn't mean it offensively, being a dyke yourself and all."

Bleu's smile melted off her face. Jasmine, who was sitting at the table across from ours', laughed loudly. She covered her mouth when the attention was focused on her.

Lily laughed, too. Avery gave me a knowing look.

"According to the lesbian handbook, page five hundred

and fifty-two," Quincy stated. "If a dyke calls another person a dyke, it's acceptable."

"Shut up, n-" And then Rachel said it.

I stood up not caring that I knocked Graham's food over in the process. I stepped out of my chair and stood in front of Rachel trying to look as intimidating as possible. Quincy looked small. Her smile dissipated like passing clouds. Avery quickly hurried behind me in alarm with a smile on her face.

Bleu tapped her foot a few times before she looked at Rachel. "You shouldn't say that."

"It was the only word that fit," Rachel said while staring me down.

Cassidy held a giggle in. I nearly charged at all three of them but Avery held me back, tucking me to her chest and resting her chin on my shoulder. She whispered 'it's not worth it' over and over again in my ear.

Quincy looked at Bleu solemnly and shrugged. She stared at her for awhile with glossy brown eyes. "You win," Quincy muttered. She took her seat beside Lily. She rested her head on her knuckle to hide her face and continued to eat. Lily rolled her eyes at Bleu and her friends. The two tables were quiet. Bleu was staring at the back of Eden's head.

Eden's eyes were burning red from the erupting lava inside her. "Why couldn't you just leave her alone?" She whispered hoarsely to Bleu. She laughed bitterly. "Why do you always have to fucking embarrass me?" She grabbed her black and orange windbreaker jacket before she left the cafeteria. If our table wasn't quiet before, you could hear a pin drop now. Bleu slowly followed her out with her head hung.

-

A text came in on my phone from Eden later that night.

Eden: *Not that I care, but my dad wants to know if you've seen Bleu.*

Me: No I haven't. Last I saw her she was following you out of the cafeteria.

Another one came in from Creep. That was Todd, Bleu's twin.

Creep: Hey, sorry to bug you. Have you seen Bleu?

I stared down at the message. I had an idea of where she could be. I grabbed my floral green jacket and ran downstairs.

"Where are you going?" Sylvia asked.

I grabbed my notebook, fumbling with my pencil. ***To see if my friend is okay. It's really important.*** I've never referred to Bleu as a friend but I don't think she'd let me go otherwise.

"Alright, just make it fast, don't get into any trouble."

I sprinted out of the house as fast I could. Half way down the block I realized it would have been more convenient if I rode there on my bike. I approached the soccer field and sure enough Bleu was at the top of the bleachers staring at nothing. I jogged all the way up the steps and looked down at her. My movement echoed around us from the contact my shoes made with the metal. She didn't even acknowledge I was there. Her face was red with translucent pale tear streaks lining them.

"I would never say that." She shook her head. "I would never say that to anyone!"

Your whole family is looking for you, I wrote but I didn't show it to her yet.

"I have to see Quincy tomorrow," she said. "She probably hates me so much now. And, God, that stupid thing I said before in the locker room?" She shook her head. "I don't even know why I said that. Quincy makes me say the most stupidest things. I have friends who say it so she probably thinks I've called her that before behind her back and … and Eden," she laughed. "Oh I give up on Eden. She hates me no matter what I do. And I mean whatever I do."

I showed her what I wrote.

She smiled. "I don't want to go home yet."

Practice the next day was awkward. Bleu was the only person giving drills on the football field while Quincy followed what she said rather than helped her. Avery stayed after school to watch me play. She wants to kiss me, I know it, but I can't do it. I held her hand as we walked home. Bleu was sulking behind us. Avery nudged me. "Aren't you worried she's gonna say something?"

I shook my head. She had bigger fish to fry. That night, Z and Bleu were talking about enigmatic shit again and I listened this time. We were all sitting in the pouring rain. My dad was out working and Sylvia still couldn't give me the time of day again. Every word she said to me was so forced that I just stopped writing back to her in general. Bleu closed her eyes and leaned back on her hands. She tilted her head up to the sky. Her hair matted against her forehead.

"Sydney doesn't know that I have freak out episodes."

"She doesn't need to know anyway." Bleu opened her eyes.

"I feel like I'm trying to impress her."

"Everyone in a relationship feels like that."

"That's probably why I don't enjoy being with her very much."

"In some relationships, you feel like you have to impress them but sometimes you get so lucky that you have fun when you do it and oftentimes impressing them is the only thing that makes you happy."

"Have you been in a relationship like that?" Z asked.

Bleu closed her eyes and smiled. "No, but I can dream."

"I know someone who can make me feel like that."

"Then why don't you go out with them?"

Z smiled and shook his head. "No. Everyone would laugh at me." He stared upwards and focused on the rain.

"We won't laugh at you. Will we?" She looked at me.

I smiled. I shook my head. "We won't laugh at you."

Z laughed. "Good."

-

"Wanna talk about this?" Sylvia asked.

I didn't speak.

"It's okay to be into women."

I know. *I know.*

She read what I wrote. "So you've been into them this whole time? Even during the..." Stop, I thought to myself. "Oh. Yeah it's okay don't answer that. And I...I didn't tell your father."

Thanks.

"I tried that kind of sex in college and it's not bad at all. It was fine. I shouldn't be telling you this. Um..." she rubbed her arms. Her voice cracked under the pressure. "There are a lot of pros when it comes to being a lesbian. Do you identify as a lesbian?"

Sure. *I guess.*

"Okay. One you can still have kids, you can still have sex, like I so awkwardly mentioned before, you can get married nowadays, you can complain about your menstrual cycle as much as you want and you don't have to get up in the morning before your spouse does so that you can freshen up and pretend you actually woke up like that."

I giggled. ***I have a girlfriend.*** Ew, why did I tell her that?

"Oh. What's her name?"

Avery Martinez. Oh my god?

"That's a nice name."

Thanks. Where's your dignity? Where's your pride?

"How long have you two been together?"

A week.

"Oh it's fresh?"

I nodded.

"Can I meet her?"

You probably think I'm making all this shit up don't you? I thought to myself. I smiled and nodded.

"Cool I'd love to."

Ten

If I told you that a flower bloomed in a dark room, would you trust it? -Kendrick Lamar

"How have you been sleeping?" William asked me. He scooted beside me on the navy blue bedspread. I shook my head. I haven't been sleeping well since Z's outburst. Every time we're alone in the living room together, I immediately get out. It hurts his feelings but I don't think things will ever be the same. "He's not going to attack you out of the blue again I promise you," he said practically reading my mind.

I'll get over it.

Then he began to stare at me. He was dying to tell me something. He had a look in his eyes. "Do you wanna talk about something?" He asked. I knew it. I only shook my head again. "I just want to know something."

Stay ignorant, I wrote.

"Mercury, what's wrong?"

Nothing. Until you barged in here.

"Tell me."

I guess I was still frustrated with myself about Avery.

I'm dating someone and we haven't kissed yet.

William nodded. "I know you feel like you're not ready

yet," he said. "But kissing doesn't have to lead to anything. Just tell them that. What's his name? Maybe I know him."

You know them.

"Who?"

Should I tell him? No, then that would be three people who know I'm gay. Word spreads fast like wildfire. "It's a girl, isn't it?"

Oh.

I just stared down at the laptop on my lap contemplating whether I should answer yes.

"That's what I wanted to know," he slowly drawled out.

I scratched my head.

"What's her name? You can tell me."

Avery.

William's eyes enlarged and a huge smile was planted on his face. "I am so proud of you. And I mean that. I really do."

I laughed. I paused before I wrote down. *I can talk to her.*

William's smile faded making me regret my decision to tell him immediately.

Don't tell anyone.

"I won't. I won't I swear. Mercury?" His mouth hung open. "That's great!"

I nodded.

"This is a lot to take in. Avery won't hurt you. She won't."

You don't know that.

"You know she won't. You and I both know she's harmless."

76

I don't know what it was about Avery that made me so ridiculously comfortable. More comfortable than how I am with my family. Telling her about my condition and how she's the only one I'm able to talk to didn't make her feel bad as much. I tried not to think about her selfish outlook on it.

Avery dangled from the yellow monkey bars.

I caught her by her waist, staring down at her glistening diamond belly button ring.

"Take a picture, Mercury." She smiled coyly. I shook my head laughing.

"Sorry." I set her down and brushed myself off. Avery was standing really close to me. "Um so what do you want to do?"

She bit her lip and sighed. "Every relationship is awkward Mercury until one person becomes extremely close to the other person. They have one thing that doesn't make their relationship seem like an average friendship. You know what I mean?"

"Yeah." I nodded, backing up into the ladder.

Avery's peridot eyes glanced down at my mouth and then back up at me. "You don't think I have syphilis do you?"

I froze. "What?"

"Or herpes?"

"What? No."

"Then why won't you kiss me?"

"Why won't *you* kiss me?" I asked trying to stall.

"Because every time I try, you get this scared look in your eyes like you just saw...Freddie Krueger."

I laughed. "I'm sorry. I haven't kissed anyone in awhile."

"Neither have I. Not since I've been around you again."

"I won't flip out this time."

"This time?"

I nodded.

Avery leaned in.

I tapped her stomach. "Tag! You're it!" I started sprinting away.

"What the hell?!"

I turned around and blew a raspberry and started taking off again. She darted full speed after me. When I looked back, my eyes widen. "Oh shit!" I exclaimed.

Avery started laughing. I made an attempt at running faster but I tripped into the wet grass. "Oh God." Avery fell on top of me giggling. "Tag." She quickly got up. "You're it." She took off jogging backwards. I got up to go after her but suddenly the sprinklers turned on full blast spraying water everywhere.

Avery halted, shocked by the sprays of water. I ran into her from behind and lifted her up. She broke into a laughing fit. Her dampened hair was flattened against her head. I set her on the ground and kept my arms wrapped around her waist, resting my chin on her shoulder.

"Have you been seeing anyone?" I asked.

"No, I haven't. I told you."

"Thanks for lying."

"I haven't." She giggled. "Honest."

"Oh."

She closed her eyes and smiled so I could look at her and she wouldn't have to know. "You don't have to kiss me now, just know..." She laid her arms back so they were wrapped around my neck. "I really like you."

I caught Jasmine on my way home. She was bounding

down the steps out of Eden's house. She was wearing a green sparkly hijab and a long sleeved brown shirt. She looked over at me and waved. "Hey you." I waved back and jogged over to her. "That was really awkward." She indicated over to Eden's house with her thumb. "I haven't spoken to Bleu in a minute."

I pulled out my notebook. ***Understandable.***

"She's getting better at Calculus," Jasmine lowered her voice. She pulled me along so that we could be far from the house. "So hopefully she won't need me anymore you know?" She shrugged. "Anyway, how's Quincy doing?"

Quincy seems fine. She still holds hands with Lily in the hallways, she's still hilarious, she's finally doing drills and warm ups again. But every time Cassidy or Rachel make a smart (usually rude) remark she just gives a pathetic smile and carries on. Everyone on the team knows what happened to Quincy in the lunchroom so no one laughs with Cassidy and Rachel, even if they already dislike Quincy. Bleu has darker circles under her eyes now a days and has been frequently unobtrusive.

I don't know, is what I wrote to Jasmine. ***She ignores the elephant in the room.***

"Poor thing. Too bad Bleu said all that to her. She seemed like a nice person."

She's just confused and it makes her mad.

"Confused?"

I shook my head, waving it off.

"I'm kind of relieved it was Rachel who said the other word and not Bleu or I would have lost a job."

Bleu's not like that.

"Yeah well. You can never be sure."

I nodded.

"I gotta go. Family dinner." She nudged me. "Wanna come?"

Why not? I had nothing better to do. And dinner with my family can't be more awkward than dinner with her family.

Sure. Let me ask my dad.

-

"Hey, everyone, this is Mercury!" I entered the room. An unstoppable smile spread across my face when I saw so many people seated at the dinner table.

"Hi, Mercury!" They all chanted. I was hit by so much love and warmth the minute I stepped into the house, I nearly said 'hello' back.

"Don't worry I told them you can't talk. One of my cousins had that mutism thing, too." I must have looked surprised because she continued, "Yeah yeah, he was in a car crash and his vocal chords weren't messed up but he was completely traumatized by the whole ordeal. It freaked my aunts and my mother out. He ended up moving out with his wife once he started talking again." I nodded seemingly interested.

"I hear he's a geometry teacher now."

Nice.

I learned Jasmine lives with four brothers, two sisters, three cousins, two aunts, two uncles, her mother and father, grandfather, grandmother, and her baby niece named Sarafina who keeps playing with my hair and whose name was the only one I could remember. Dinner was amazing. Usually I'm not one to try new foods because of my food sensitivity, but I don't regret giving it a try. I also ended up learning that Jasmine and her family were from Egypt. Jasmine was born in Cairo which her siblings are jealous of. Or so she says. We had Egyptian rice with Vermicelli noodles, phyllo meat pies, feteer meshaltet (cheesy pastries) and my favorite, molokhia, which tastes a lot like okra, over rice. The whole table spoke Arabic when arguing with one another and English when they were calm.

When dinner was over, Jasmine's little brothers and cousins were running all over the house. Her mother and her aunt picked up an argument they were going at throughout the dinner. The men were laughing and chatting with booming voices echoing throughout the house. They made their way over to the living room to watch tv.

The beautiful quiet sister that sat next to me during dinner smiled politely at me as she collected plates from the table. She went into the kitchen to help her grandmother washing the dishes. I stared at her butt when she went in and I think Jasmine caught me.

She brought me into her room after I put my plate in the sink. A little girl was sitting on the floor. "Get out of my room," Jasmine said to her. She was brushing a Bratz doll's hair. She was the only girl that wasn't dressed in a hijab and longed sleeved shirts.

"What?" She whined. "This is my room, too."

"Now," she said firmly.

Her sister's face scrunched up as if she was about to cry and she stormed out of the bedroom. Jasmine closed the door behind them. "I'm not homophobic or anything," she started.

Uh oh. A sentence starting like that, never ends well.

"But I know you're gay so please don't hit on me." She grabbed a lollipop from inside her top dresser drawer. "Want a Dum Dum?"

That was four people who knew I was gay now.

I wrote, **why does everyone assume I'm gay?**

"Are you kidding?" she asked amidst a laugh.

I shook my head.

"I don't know." She laid down on her bed. "I guess it's the way you look. The eyebrow ring, the Yankees hat, the black jacket."

I narrowed my eyes.

"You just look gay. I can't explain it."

You're so sure that I'm a lesbian because of how I dress?

She nodded. "Aren't you gay?"

Maybe. Do you think Avery's gay?

"Hmm I don't know."

You're kidding? I thought to myself.

"And the way you walk."

I snorted. **Show me.**

Jasmine shrugged. She took slow steps twisting her shoulders side to side exaggeratedly as she walked. I laughed louder than normal and roughly shoved her back on her bed. "That's what you do," she said defensively.

I walked across the room.

"Yup." She demonstrated again. I haven't laughed this much in so long.

Saturday morning, I was still thinking about my trip to Jasmine's house. I wanted a family like that. I knew I would enjoy coming home to a large group of people who you could talk to about anything. I went to my gym near her house to clear my head. I was running on the treadmill when I caught sight of Avery. She entered the gym dressed in a red sports bra and small red shorts. God, she really loves that color. My heart started beating faster.

Gleefully, I turned the treadmill up a notch so that I was nearly sprinting now like a cheetah after it's prey. Avery walked over and curiously eyed a burly man doing sit ups with his trainer on a black mat near the weights. He had a mini black barbell in his hand. Avery said something I couldn't make out and the trainer started laughing. Avery kept on making the trainer and the guy laugh harder. Avery joined in. My heart stopped. The cheetah watched the gazelle take off 1000 feet ahead of them.

Avery gripped the guy in training's arm as he stood up off the ground. She was still in a laughing fit. She took the weight from the guy and showed that she can lift it making both of them laugh again.

I turned off the treadmill and headed into the locker room past Avery. I didn't know what to feel.

Avery spotted me. "Hey, Mercury."

I swerved past her and didn't look her way.

"Excuse me." She left the guys, following me into the locker room. "Hey. You didn't see me or something?"

I calmly looked at her and then grabbed my buried keys and the white towel on top of it.

She bit her lip. Her smile fell off her face. "Really?"

I nodded. I slammed the locker closed with a loud bang and headed out.

Avery grabbed my hand. "Mercury," she said. "Do you remember what I said?" She gave a reassuring smile. I mocked her smile and snatched my hand back. I left the gym and into the frigid air. "I know you need your space." She let a man pass her. She apologized to a woman and her kids that she nearly ran into. I kept aiming for my bike. "But I can't give you space where you're mad at me."

I laughed bitterly.

"Whatever, Mercury, I'm trying. What are you doing? You act like I just kissed someone else in front of you."

"When you understand that you don't have to put on a flirtatious act for every hot guy you come across, we'll be okay." I sat down on my bike trying to ignore the fact that I sounded like Eden. She shook her head biting her lips but an angry look coalesced in her eyes. "Estas lleno de mierda." She punched my shoulder. I biked off.

"Remember Jack?" Jasmine asked me later. We were on our walk back from the boardwalk. When she asked me if I wanted to stop by her house again, I caved. "We're going on our first date tomorrow. It's a surprise. I'm telling my family I'm going to your house."

Clever.

Jasmine smiled.

"Hey, Jasmine." I rolled my eyes.

"Oh hey, Avery. We were just heading back to my place wanna come?" Why is Jasmine so nice?

I looked away from Avery. I rubbed the bruise she made on my shoulder.

"I have a therapy group thing in an hour so I gotta head down there but can I talk to Mercury for a second? Just a second."

"Uh sure." Jasmine gave a discouraged smile and walked ahead. I didn't look at Avery.

"I'll do whatever you want. Whatever you want for you to forgive me." Avery gripped the guy's bicep over and over again in my head. "Name anything. And I'll do it. God, I'll do anything you want."

Leave me alone.

Avery looked at Jasmine and then back at me. "Do you like her?"

I frowned confused.

"Jasmine?"

I shook my head slowly.

Avery laughed. "Okay, 'been to her house before?"

I rolled my eyes again.

"Just answer," She said. I nodded. "Well strike one."

We're not tied, asshole.

"You were jealous and now I'm jealous. It's fair."

I scoffed. **Nice try.** I looked back at Jasmine and then back at Avery before I wrote. ***And I do like her a little bit.***

Avery stared up at me. When she didn't react, I shrugged and followed Jasmine.

Eleven

Your name is the strongest positive and negative connotation in any language. It either lights me up or leaves me aching for days.

• Rupi Kaur

"I'm going to a party tonight," Eden said. She was wearing the Tupac t-shirt I got her for her birthday last year. She was fixing her hair in the mirror. She tried putting it in a puffy ponytail. She sighed and put her hands on her hips. "Large hoop earrings will balance this out."

I smiled while chewing my gum. *Up your status.*

Eden laughed. "Yusuf is gonna be there."

I winked and pretended to nudge her. Eden laughed. "You're silly. I'll text you everything once I get there. See ya. I'm so late, bye."

I waved and headed back over to my room across the roof. I closed the window shut behind me. I turned the volume back up on my TV. Seinfeld was on. I heard a knock. To my right outside the window was Avery. Even though she caught me staring at her, she knocked again. I muted the TV and opened the window.

"Did you read over what you wrote to me yesterday?" She asked.

I blinked. Only one hundred times, I thought to myself. I didn't move a muscle. Avery sighed irritatedly, "I slept with someone last night," she said rashly.

My heart crashed and the shattered pieces were at my feet. "Good for you."

Avery nodded. "It was good for me. I'm sure it was for him, too." She smiled and folded her arms.

"You know," I whispered. "I was worried that you were gonna hurt me. That's why I was so afraid to kiss you. William told me you weren't going to but I knew that somehow you were going to. I just didn't know how. But now I do." I smiled. "So thank you, Avery, for helping my stance."

"Everyone is going to hurt you in life, Mercury. Everyone. I didn't even mean to hurt you."

"I know," I said matter-of-factly. "And that's the worst part."

It became dead silent before she said, "I love you."

That made me laugh the way my dad does when the Italian in him breaks loose during a discussion. "Oh give me a break."

"I do. I love you. I'm madly in love with you. Every time I see you, I think about you afterwards for 24 hours. It's disgusting. Everything I do, I think about whether you would like me doing it or not. 'What would Mercury want me to do?'"

"Everything you do, huh? Was that before or after yesterday?"

"Both. And I know you love me, too."

"Enlighten me."

"You're talking to me!"

I stopped and took a breath. There was a golden halo emanating from above her head from the sunset. Her hair strands danced with the wind from the chilly air. We were stuck in a pause due to a broken remote.

"Do you talk to other people?" She gesticulated breathing heavily. "Do you talk to Jasmine?"

"No?"

"So? So you love..." She stared at the floor. She looked back up at me. Her lips parted but I interjected before she could say anything.

"Doesn't matter now," I said.

"Yeah." Both of us were quiet. "It's cold out here."

I moved out the way for her to come in. She climbed in and laid back against the window. "Nice room."

As if things couldn't get any worse, Sylvia decided to come in. "Mercury, can I borrow your scissors? Oh, hi."

"Hi," Avery said meekly.

"Hi," Sylvia said again. "Are you Avery?" God.

"Uh yeah." Avery smiled back and scratched her cheek. "How'd you know?"

"I've heard a lot about you."

I grabbed the large blue scissors and handed them to her.

"Alright alright I'm going. Nice meeting you, Avery."

"Nice meeting you, too."

Sylvia left.

"You told your mom about me." She sat against the wall clutching her stomach. Her face was turning green.

"She's not my mom." I stared at her. I knelt down to her level. "You don't love me."

Avery shook her head. "Stop thinking you're the wisest

person on Earth okay? You don't know everything. Some things, I am sure about."

I leaned closer and kissed her cheek. I didn't feel good about it.

Avery blushed scarlet.

Good party? I asked Eden.

Eden shook her head.

Oh.

Eden put the top hat on top of my head of pink hair. "You look like a magician."

I smiled. Eden shot me a weak smile back.

I'm sorry. I wrote it out so fast, I practically blurted it out.

"For what?" Eden asked.

I was holding tears in the back of my throat. I wrote, *I don't know.*

"I've been seeing a psychiatrist and she's been helping me a lot. She says I have to get back out there." She giggled. "As if I'm some middle aged woman who's divorced with two kids and working for a newspaper."

I chuckled.

"I like her," Eden said. She's nice."

Good.

"It's not because of you."

My whole body frosted over.

"Not that you were...pondering the possibility of this being because of you. It's not because of you at all."

Yes it is. It's okay, I shakily wrote.

"It's not."

A tear escaped my eye.

89

Eden put the hat back. She pulled me by the arm outside the store. "Consistently, I've been really depressed thinking my life has no substance anymore. And that life is gonna be an endless cycle of watching people be happy, charismatic and proficient with their lives but thinking 'I wish that was me' every time. It's made me ill that's all." Eden wiped my eyes with her sweater sleeve.

Do you know I love you? I didn't look up to see if she read it.

"Yeah, freak. I'm much better now. Can't you tell?"

Yeah. No.

"I love you, too. You look brighter, what's been going on with you lately? You're like a ray of um, I don't know. What's pink and bright? Forget it. What's up?"

I tried to think up a lie. My hesitancy was obvious and Eden sighed.

"It's okay if it's Avery. I'm happy for us, either way."

Twelve

Reality is wrong. Dreams are for real.

• **Tupac Shakur**

Bleu and I were walking in silence to the soccer field. Eden had texted me informing me that Bleu wanted to talk to me and that Bleu said I knew what she meant. Beats me why Bleu didn't feel comfortable on the walk to the field, but I didn't want to poke her and find out why. She was staring at the cracks in the sidewalk trying not to step on any of them. Once we got there, there were two people already there lying in the grass. I spotted Lily and Quincy before Bleu. Bleu stopped in her tracks. "We should turn back," Bleu suggested. I shrugged. I didn't really care either way. "I don't think she's a dyke," she said. "I mean I know Quincy's gay but I don't think she's a dyke. I don't have anything against people being gay." She started babbling. I nodded.

"We can talk out here. Yeah?" Bleu folded her arms trying not to look past the fence. I nodded again.

"Hey!"

Bleu jumped and glanced over at Lily coming over to us. "Get the fuck outta here!"

"I was just-"

"No. I don't wanna hear it. Just go." She looked at me and gave a discourteous scowl. "You, too."

I raised an eyebrow. 'The fuck did I do?

"She didn't do anything," Bleu said. "Leave her alone."

"Leave *us* alone then. What are you so afraid of anyway? You think Q likes you or something because she doesn't. It's all in your conceited little head. She doesn't like you. In fact, she kind of hates you now. How does it feel to not have someone be head over heels for you, Bleu?" She pushed Bleu. Bleu nearly tripped over her own two feet and closed her eyes.

"Go." Lily turned around and mumbled. "Need a restraining order." She went back over to Quincy who was standing up looking at Bleu with curious wide eyes.

"Why'd she kiss me then?" Bleu asked me.

I didn't mean to smile but I did. I looked at the ground.

Lily turned around. "Excuse me?"

Bleu's eyes fell back on Lily. "She kissed me in front of you, remember? She paid me."

Lily flared her nostrils. She came over to her. "Say that again. I didn't hear you."

Bleu looked over at me.

My bottom lip protruded out as I gave a smile. Lily laughed derisively. She went into punch her but I stopped her fist with the palm of my hand.

"Woah woah." Quincy jogged up to us. She broke Lily and I apart and wrapped an arm around my shoulders. "No need to fight."

"Can you tell her to leave?" Lily asked she tucked her black hair behind her ear. "Please."

Bleu was a little shaken up over almost getting knocked out. She stared at Quincy with wide eyes. "Yeah, Quincy, tell me to leave."

Quincy wouldn't even look Bleu in the eye. She looked over at Lily and winked. "It's freezing let's get out of here." Lily complied with a small smile so fast you'd think she was put under a spell. Quincy wrapped an arm around her shoulder. They calmly headed back the way we came.

"I'm sorry I called you two dykes," Bleu called out.

They kept walking.

"It was immature."

"Sorry I almost sent you on your ass." Lily laughed. She wasn't actually apologizing.

"It's fine," Bleu said anyway. Quincy averted her eyes back over to me. Her smile faded. She was probably just now realizing I'm actually hanging out with Bleu. I looked at Bleu and then back at her and nodded subtly. Quincy pulled Lily closer and kept walking. As their silhouettes faded, Bleu said to me, "Stuart wants to sleep with me."

Suddenly, it felt like the sidewalk dipped and I grabbed the wire fence for dear life. "Oh my god. Mercury, are you okay?"

I nodded. I kept gripping the fence.

"I told him I wasn't ready. God," She shook her head. "He's probably thinking about leaving me. The last thing I need right now is Stuart leaving me. I'm such an idiot. But I don't think I can do it. I can't open myself up like that to just anyone. Literally. Not that Stuart's just anyone but...all he does is football, kiss me, and occasionally takes me to eat at Mickey D's or something."

I let go of the fence but my legs still trembled with

weakness. I grabbed it again. My face reddening with embarrassment. I covered my face with the palm of my hand.

"I'm gonna take you home," Bleu said. I could tell she was trying to seem unfazed by my predicament. "Alright?" I nodded slowly.

Bleu wrapped my arm around her shoulder and held my side as we were walking to get me home.

Once we reached my house, we spotted Quincy sitting on Bleu's white wooden porch steps. She was dark under no lighting. "I would never call you that word," Bleu said immediately.

Quincy blinked.

"I would never call you that!" She pointed a finger at Quincy still holding on to my side. "Ever!"

Quincy howled with laughter. "Whatever." She rubbed her eyes in frustration. "Just drop it."

"I need you to tell me you know that."

Quincy looked up at her and scoffed. "You don't need me to tell you anything," Quincy said.

"Rachel's a complete idiot."

"Then why are you friends with her?!" Quincy stood up.

"There's no point in leaving new people right now."

Quincy scrunched her face up. "What?"

"You don't get it. Okay? You don't get it because y-you're free and you don't care if people judge you. Everyone loves you. Everyone loves Quincy." Quincy shook her head in disbelief. "You think I don't know that everyone says they hate me only to act fake around me." Bleu continued smiling. "Because I'm so pretty, because I have all these tight-ass friends. I know.

94

My sister is your friend. I don't hear the end of it from her at home and I don't need to hear from anyone else."

"I don't have the energy to hear you feeling sorry for yourself," Quincy said.

"You're the one sitting outside my house!"

"You shouldn't have called me a dyke or none of this would have happened. That really broke me."

"Well don't do PDA where people have to eat."

"You're so pathetic."

"You pity me?"

"Yeah. Your life is so dull and sad that you find a fascination in mine."

"So you're sad but I'm extra sad?"

"Exactly."

Bleu scoffed. "Tell me something I don't know."

"You had two moms and they both died. So maybe you don't know this but you're not just sad, you're unlucky, too."

Quincy threw a bolt of lightning at me. She doused me in gasoline and lit a match for Bleu only to throw it on me. Overcome with anger, I instantaneously grabbed a few rocks from the soil above ground and chucked it at Quincy's chest. Quincy attempted to dodge them and winced. I couldn't stop chucking them at her over and over again. Every time I threw a rock, I was seeing my crayon sketched drawings of a woman holding a baby next to a boy with long brown hair and a round cheery man. Sometimes, I think I'm an animal at the zoo and my mom is on the opposite side of the blurry glass. I'm banging against the glass but the woman who could be my mother just smiles at me and waves through it. That's the dream I always have when Z has a fit.

Bleu held onto me tightly and we inevitably fell to the

ground. I didn't realize until a tear made its way to my lips that I was bawling.

Quincy was shaking. "I'm sorry, Bleu. I'm sorry, Mercury I wasn't thinking."

"It's fine," Bleu said. "See Mercury? She was just angry. She didn't mean it." I couldn't hear myself crying. I felt like I was in a dream drawing a perfect mother in purple crayon.

"I'm sorry," Quincy said again. She was about to cry but turned around before we could see her and quickly left the scene.

Thirteen

If you always put limits on everything you do, physical or anything else, it will spread into your work and into your life. There are no limits. There are only plateaus, and you must not stay there, you must go beyond them.

- **Bruce Lee**

Jack took a seat to the right of Jasmine and I in math class. "Hi," Jasmine said.

"Hi," he said.

Jasmine nodded and kept nodding before she broke into a fit of laughter. "I'm sorry I didn't even know you were in this class."

"Clearly, I was just transferred into this class."

Jasmine furrowed her eyebrows "When?"

"Today?" Jack said.

"Ohhhh." She gave a bright white smile. "Okay." She pointed to me. "You remember Mercury."

"'Sup." He smiled at me.

"So Jack, are you going to the championship soccer game tonight?" Jasmine asked. "Mercury's playing."

"I don't know. Are you?" He asked.

"Yeah."

"Then yes." I rolled my eyes, pointed to my open mouth and gagged. Jasmine caught me.

"Oh shut up." She whacked my head with her folder before I could get to her first.

Quincy sat down awkwardly next to me. She was dressed in a black blazer and black dress pants with "The Amazing World of Gumball" t-shirt underneath. I focused on the 'do now' math problems on the board and attempted to solve them. Even though I didn't understand any of it, I made it look like I did. "Mercury," she said. She leaned closer to me. "First planet from the sun, Hg, I'm sorry. I completely forgot. I don't know what it's like to not know your mom. I knew mine but I don't think my parents would ever let me see her again. I don't think I want to either. And I don't remember what it's like to actually have the desire to see her."

I nodded. I suddenly felt selfish for making her feel bad. *It's okay,* is all I wrote.

"I wanted to make Bleu cry," she admitted to me. "And I just transformed into this monster. I was also feeling confused. What were you two hanging out for anyway? I thought you and I were on the same wavelength when it came to Bleu."

That's confidential. Even though we didn't get a chance to talk about Quincy.

"Oh. Well she wasn't in my first period. English. I kind of hope she's okay."

You should.

She looked up at me showing compunction. She fidgeted in her chair. She tapped the eraser of her pencil against the table. "Maybe she was late."

Maybe.

I glanced over at the girl with thick shoulder length scarlet red hair and scarlet painted lips to match. Her green peridot eyes glistened from the reflection of the dim afternoon sun peeking out from the glass windows in the hallway. "Where are you headed?"

I smiled. With teeth. We just secretly started seeing each other again. I'm not sure I should be giving the all teeth smile just yet. I opened the black leather notebook in my hand and took the pencil out of the rings of the notebook. *The elevator*, I wrote.

Avery frowned. "What's wrong with the stairs?" She jerked her thumb back at a bunch of rowdy students heading out the ugly beige door and down the flight of stairs.

There's too many.

Avery laughed heartily and shook her head. I watched Eden awkwardly walk ahead of us.

The three of us stood in front of the elevator. The school was booming with noise from the students yet it seemed like all the sound was escaping through a black hole. Eden placed a folded up kente cloth from her bag onto her head.

It takes a while for the elevator to reach the second floor because so many students use it now. It's a wide elevator that took the school over 5 months to build. It can hold up to more than 12 students.

"Can't I drive you home and then drive you back to your car?" A firm masculine voice tore through my head. I began feeling lightheaded again. I stepped forward, closer to the elevator. I slowly glanced behind me and expectedly I caught sight of a familiar boy dressed in a varsity black and yellow letterman jacket with the last name Green on the back. He had his arm gently wrapped around Bleu who wasn't wearing the varsity jacket anymore. The girl with long golden curls cascading down her back was in a white see-through button down shirt, denim shorts, and wearing black sunglasses.

"I guess that would make sense in your world," Bleu replied reassuringly.

The boy sighed. "I would've picked you up if I noticed you were late but I got here at 7:58."

"Stuart it's fine. Tell you what, come to my house later. Around eight-ish…"

"Hey, Stuart." A heavy set black kid named Tyrone waved him over.

"See you, tonight." Stuart bent down to kiss her. He looked down and smiled before he jogged over to Tyrone. I breathed out a long sigh of relief, counting my blessings that he didn't catch sight of me.

Bleu stood behind Avery, who I just realized was looking at me concerned.

Jasmine approached Bleu. "Hey, Bleu."

"Oh uh hey…Jasmine," Bleu said attempting to remember her name.

I looked over at Eden. She was wearing her "I Met God. She's Black" shirt and had a just-as-surprised look on her face. Jasmine started fidgeting as Bleu waited for her to say something. "Since I'm coming over to your house at 3, I thought it'd be easier if I just came with you. You have a car right?"

"Yeah," Bleu said. "It's just I usually get situated first before I bring people over. And I kind of made plans today um I'm sorry. I was gonna tell you."

"It's fine." Jasmine scratched her head while staring at her shoes. I directed my gaze back over at Eden again.

Eden subtly shook her head at Bleu's actions and rolled her eyes while chewing her gum obnoxiously. When I say subtle, I mean subtle for Eden. Bleu clearly saw Eden's reaction and visibly had the urge to break her streak of not talking to her sister at school but instead just started texting. Probably about how annoying certain people in school are to Stuart.

The elevator doors finally opened. I entered first and stood by the opposite corner. I watched the others file in. No one's head was in it. They entered like zombies thinking about a hundred things at once. I know I was.

"None of you are supposed to be in here," Eden said.

"When have they ever said we couldn't be in here?" Bleu said.

"This elevator is for medical reasons and staff only," Eden retorted. "Weren't you there for freshman orientation?"

"Physically, never mentally."

Eden muttered. "That's what I thought."

"Well what the hell are you doing in here then?" Avery said.

Eden continued to chew her gum with the prominent unwavering gaze she was shooting at Avery. Avery looked away. Target: intimidated.

The elevator doors were about to close when Quincy instantly stuck her hand out and it opened it back up. She gave a small warm smile as she entered. She cheerily stood by Avery. "Sup, Avery?" she said with her deep soothing voice. She gave a small nod over at me. "Mercury."

I waved. Quincy ruffled my thick pink hair softly. I'll never get tired of that.

Bleu immediately avoided Quincy's gaze and stared at the tiled floor.

"Any of you know where the library is?" Quincy asked.

"You've never been to the school library?"

"I never had a reason to go."

Jasmine chuckled. Quincy winked at her.

"The biggest room in the whole school and you can't find it?" Avery asked. "It's the end of the day why do you need to go to the library anyway?"

"I need to get this book my class started reading while I was out... "sick"." She made finger quotes.

"That sucks. What's it about?"

"How the fuck am I supposed to know I didn't read it yet?"

Jasmine chuckled again.

Quincy gave a small smile at her. It was immediately wiped off her face when she caught sight of Bleu.

The elevator began to descend but then it came to an abrupt stop making Eden and I crash into the corner walls of the elevator and everyone else fall forward. Avery's eyes widened igniting the whites of them. "What the fuck was that?"

"Oh shit." Eden's voice rose an octave. "We're not moving."

"Give it a minute," Jasmine said calmly. The room was filled with a thick silence. A couple minutes later, we all started to flip out.

Eden pressed the red call button. The button made a loud dial tone sound that got deeper as time passed until it shut off entirely. Eden pressed it again and again. Nothing.

Quincy started laughing. She folded her hands and rested them on top of her head. "This is a great day back."

Bleu pressed the open and close buttons repetitively. "Shit!"

"Aw man." Jasmine leaned back against the wall and closed her eyes. "I think I'm gonna be sick."

"No!" The girls exclaimed.

"Here." Quincy reached into her pocket. "I have mint flavored gum. Takes away the nausea." She handed it over to her.

Bleu pulled her phone out and frantically tapped at her screen. "There's no service in here."

Everyone began checking their phone as well.

"Crap." Eden roughly hit the buttons with her palm.

"This is not the way I wanna go out," Avery stated.

"We're not dying in here," Bleu stated.

"It's the end of the school day," Avery said. "No one's gonna realize the elevator is broken until tomorrow."

"We have Bleu, though," Eden reassured us. "People will realize we're missing."

Bleu glared at Eden. "You are really starting to annoy me now."

"I'm just saying since you know a lot of people, people will realize you're missing and ask around."

"She's right." Quincy began to smile. "Your posse won't be able to make it without you for at least a good hour or two."

Bleu stuck up the middle finger. I figured we'd be in here awhile so I slid down the wall and onto the white tile floor. I looked up at everyone frantically pacing the elevator.

"I'm really not good in small spaces," Jasmine said.

"Pretend you're in your room right now," Avery responded. She looked around. Her red hair began to dance from the humidity of the elevator. "And none of this is real."

My messages to my father still weren't sending out. Bleu attempted to call her dad but the call dropped. "Great."

"What if we run out of oxygen or something?"

"Shut up, Eden." Bleu mimicked me and sat on the ground. "Can you do that for one second? Use Mercury as an example."

Eden scoffed. Quincy smiled. "Wow way to be a dick, Bleu."

"I wasn't talking to you. When someone's not talking to you, you don't say anything. Plain and simple."

Quincy rose her eyebrows in shock. "Yes ma'am."

Jasmine giggled.

"Wow." Bleu sympathetically smiled over at Jasmine. "Cory was right, you do find everything amusing."

Jasmine smile faded. This was gonna be interesting.

Fourteen

Whenever you find yourself on the side of the majority, it is time to pause and reflect.

- **Mark Twain**

Forty minutes went by. We were all sitting on the floor. Quincy was eating leftover ziti out of a clear container.

"We should probably establish some small talk," Quincy said with her mouth full. "Seeing it's been almost an hour now. Um." She placed her hand against her chest. "I'm Quincy. Some of my friends call me Q."

"Hi Quincy." Avery said slowly in a monotonous tone of voice. Quincy rolled her eyes.

"Ha. Ha." Quincy poked her in her cheek with her index finger and twisted it.

"I'm Eden. This is Mercury."

"I'm Jasmine."

"Avery."

"Bleu."

"Well that was stupid," Quincy said. "I already know all of you."

"No one calls you Q, Quincy," Bleu said.

"You just did."

Jasmine sat up straight. "Q, what'd you get on that math test?"

Quincy looked up. "Thanks for putting me on the spot, Jasmine."

"Just making small talk."

"It's fine I got a 79."

"Oh."

"She said condescendingly," Quincy muttered.

"That test was kind of hard," Avery helped. "Math is a pain in the ass."

"Not when you sit next to June Matthews."

"You and June Matthews, I swear."

"She's a bitch," Bleu stated matter-of-factly.

"She is but she's a nice bitch," Quincy said.

"That's true." Avery nodded.

Bleu frowned. "What?"

"There are three types of bitches," Quincy explained. "Fake bitches, nice bitches and mean bitches. Nice bitches are mean when they're with their friends but if you drop your food on the floor they'll help you pick it up. Mean bitches: Bleu is the prime example." Everyone snickered. Bleu proceeded to listen.

"Fake bitches are the worst. They're cruel and they'll act nice but even when you're alone with them they'll trash you."

"What's the difference between a fake bitch and a mean bitch?" Bleu asked.

"Mean bitches are just mean but you can hold a conversation with them."

"You learn something new everyday," Bleu said sarcastically.

"We should check our phones again," Avery said. Everyone pulled out their phones in sync.

"Ooh ooh I got something." Bleu put her phone to her ear. "Dad! Dad, hello?" Bleu removed the phone from her ear. She stared down at it. "The call dropped."

"What's it like to have sex with a woman?" Avery asked Quincy. I started feeling really hot and began perspiring. I took off my jacket.

"God." Bleu rubbed her temples. Jasmine bit her bottom lip to keep her laughter in.

"What? I wanna know."

"I don't," Eden said.

"I don't know it just happens," Quincy said. "It's a blur."

"How's the girl you're seeing?" Avery wiggles her eyebrows.

"She's... something."

"Good?" Avery asked. I want to get out of here now.

"Great. I don't like her like that entirely, though, you know? But everyone knows who I like."

"June?" Bleu asked.

"July actually. Yes, June."

"She's pretty," Jasmine stated.

"Yeah. Do you think she's-"

She raised her hands up. "Don't look at me. I don't know."

Quincy scoffed. "The con of being a lesbian." That sounds like something Sylvia would say.

The elevator eventually appeared more spacious. My eyes were a camera zooming out. Expanding as the minutes rolled by like the universe. My nerves wore me out. I wearily glanced over at Jasmine. She had a black marble notebook set out on her lap.

"What are you doing?" Bleu asked.

"Homework," Jasmine said still looking down.

"Girl, you are in the middle of a life or death situation and you're doing homework?" Eden asked.

"I doubt this constitutes as a life or death situation," Jasmine said. "And you don't have Gallagher, okay?"

"Why the hell are you taking AP English?" Avery asked.

"Looks good for college. The homework's easy though."

"What is it? Let me see." She sat next to her and grabbed the paper. "In light of our new in class novel, Lord of the Flies, I want you to construct 20 things you're scared of." Avery laughed.

"What if you aren't scared of anything?" Quincy asked.

"You make something up, Einstein."

"Oh yeah?" Quincy looked at Jasmine. "What'd you write, Jas?"

"It's personal."

"Oh c'mon we're practically family."

Jasmine narrowed her eyes. "Right."

"I can't speak for Bleu but we won't tell a soul."

Avery's eyes read over everything Jasmine had written. "It's cool. You don't have to share."

Jasmine smiled.

I know what I would write:

1. Avery. (Someone you see that's beautiful and they think you're just as beautiful are the ones you have to look out for because they will hurt you. They will.)
2. Love. (Self-explanatory)
3. Spiders. (They're everywhere. Some of them climb into your mouth when you're asleep. They have 8 legs like...how excessive is that?)

4. Balloons popping.
5. Boys. (Unpredictable species)
6. Depression. (I've been there. It's hard to get out. It's like a tidal wave; it pulls you in. When you try to swim to shore, you get hit with another one. You try to recover from the blow but you get hit by another one and you're inevitably pulled in some more.)
7. Zachariah. (You never know when he's upset or when he's really happy)
8. Eden when she's mad at me.
9. Sarafina (Jasmine's baby niece) when she's mad at me.
10. William giving up on Zachariah and I.
11. Clowns. (Creepy sons of bitches. Just watch the movie "IT".)
12. HIV. (Leads to aids.)
13. AIDS. (Leads to death.)
14. CANCER. (Leads to death/ just knowing you have it can kill you with the placebo effect)
15. Sydney when Zachariah isn't around. (She glares at me longer than what's healthy)
16. Wheat bugs. (I once almost ate cereal with a bunch of wheat bugs in it)
17. Standing in the middle of a basketball court while people are playing. (I'm prone to being hit by basketballs)
18. Time. (Too fast and sometimes too slow)
19. Getting attached to people. (Just like Avery, people who know things about you, are automatically not trustworthy. Trust no one)
20. Not being taken seriously. (I think everyone's scared of that)

Fifteen

Your time is limited, so don't waste it living someone else's life. Don't be trapped by dogma - which is living with the results of other people's thinking. Don't let the noise of others' opinions drown out your own inner voice. And most important, have the courage to follow your heart and intuition.

- **Steve Jobs**

Of the many traits that make up a person, six are now visible within these four walls: desire, regret, trepidation, capitulation, sense of amusement, and euphoria. I am the embodiment of trepidation, Avery is desire, Quincy expresses her sense of amusement constantly, Bleu lives her life regretting, Eden shows capitulation every time someone comes after her sister, and Jasmine is always happy.

Bleu's voice cut through my thoughts. "I'm sorry. It's going to bug me if I don't ask. What the hell happened to you?"

"She was the last person on Earth you've left alone," Eden's voice rose.

Bleu frowned at Eden. "You don't know?"

"I don't wanna know. It's none of my business and it sure as hell isn't yours."

"You're taking advantage of your friend instead of solving the problem. She won't talk at all."

"She's mute, smart ass," Quincy spoke up. "It's not that she won't talk, she can't talk. Eden can't do anything about that and neither can you."

"So, like I said before, how did that happen and how can we reverse it?"

"Reverse it? Missy Elliot, it's a speech disorder."

"Well she can get better can't she?"

"Sure. I don't know. I think either her voice box was damaged or she was traumatized. I read about it somewhere." I tensed up. Everyone began to stare at me except for Avery. "Right?"

"You don't have to answer that," Eden said. She was eating a Babybel cheese and playing with the red wax covering.

I looked into Avery's soft green eyes. I felt safer whenever I did that.

"What is it?" Eden asked Avery.

"What?"

"Well she keeps looking over at you."

Avery shrugged.

"Do you know about what happened to her?"

"It's none of your business. Didn't you say that?" Avery asked. "She probably doesn't want us to talk about it so let's all just drop it."

Eden was angry. Her nostrils flared like rockets. "Was it you? Did you do something to her?"

Everyone was staring at her now. "No."

"Then tell me."

Avery shook her head. "I don't have to do anything."

Eden stood up. "Tell me now."

I shook my head and tugged on Eden's shirt. She only ignored me. "No I wanna know what happened so just tell me."

Jasmine looked between the two of them. "It's probably personal, Eden."

Avery stared at the ground.

"Tell me," Eden roughly kicked her shin and a single tear trickled down Avery's face as if Eden kicked the tears she was holding in. Memories flooded into my mind like a busted dam that couldn't withstand anymore pressure. My mind raced back to a dark bedroom. Loud rock music was seeping through the walls like mold. My head was pounding. I screamed until I didn't feel it in my chest. I felt my cries for help in my heart. Blood trickled down my leg. I felt my pulsing veins in someone else's hands. My head started vibrating spastically. I broke into an intense cry that echoed off the four walls surrounding us. I covered my face but I ironically couldn't mute my hysteria. I felt a hand on me. I moved away but it was only Eden trying to calm me down.

"Well her voice box isn't broken," Quincy said.

"Shut up!" Avery exclaimed.

Quincy jumped.

"What happened, Avery?" Eden asked.

"She-" Avery wiped her face. "She doesn't want me to share."

Eden harshly grabbed her by her red collar. She shook Avery harshly, begging her to confess to what happened.

Avery began to sob. She told them. She hesitantly looked over at Bleu. Everyone stared at Bleu in shock and dismay.

Bleu stood up. "That's a bullshit lie. That's a fucking lie! Who told you that?!" I tried to quiet myself by muffling the sound with the palm of my hand. Bleu directed her gaze over at me. "God you are so full of shit. I mean I knew there was something off about you. Freshman year, I can tell you always wanted attention. You're...you're an attention whore."

Eden shoved her away. "Shut up, Bleu!"

"It's like...you need it. Like you crave it. When you used to talk, I remember you would pass out these stupid fliers the minute you entered the building every morning or make these announcements about those stupid clubs that only four people would want to go to and two people would show up to about saving the tree frogs or never eating anything with glucose in it again. It was so embarrassing because that's how pathetic you were. You'd always broadcast the most annoying shit every single day. If this lie keeps you quiet, then by all means keep sharing it." The tension enlarged. Bleu was breathing heavily using up the limited supply of air.

"You're really sad," Jasmine stated. "You know that?"

Bleu was taken aback by Jasmine's outburst. "Oh I'm sad? I haven't spoken all year to prove a point and I'm sad?"

"Yes," Avery said.

Bleu turned to Avery and laughed. "Don't even get me started on you. You are a mess!"

"What *about* me? You don't even know me."

"I know you've slept with every person in this school with a penis. I know you've taken every drug there is more

113

than three times a day. It's like you're trying to kill yourself and wanna make sure everyone knows based off the bullshit that you do."

"So what?! My life is hell and sure everyone thinks I'm a part time junkie part time slut. I know what I'm doing is wrong but never in my life have I looked at myself and then looked at you and thought 'I wish I was Bleu' because every time I see you, I feel sorry for your stuck up ass only because I thought you wanted people to know you were Ms. Thing so bad you'd amount to anything even if it meant being in a relationship with a rapist!" Avery caught her breath.

Bleu instantly went pale. She was ghost white. The elevator became quiet once again.

"Stuart was drunk at his party," Avery said in a gentler tone. "He was talking about Mercury all night. He took her upstairs to show her around. The sick son of the bitch wouldn't stop. And I tried to get her away but he kept knocking me onto the ground. He eventually broke my arm. Mercury was bleeding everywhere. If it wasn't for William Monteith, we both would have been screwed. He beat the shit out of him." Avery was clutching her hair whilst staring at the door. "I-I wanted Will to kill him. But he just walked us home after."

I looked over at Quincy who was staring at her shoes and for the first time, was speechless. Eden pushed the hair off my face and laid my head down in her lap, running her thumb down my cheek. Bleu folded her arms backing into the corner. "I still don't believe you."

"Not everyone is really how they appear to be."

Bleu shook her head. Her eyes focused in on me again. "S-she probably faked the whole thing."

Avery lunged at her but Quincy intercepted and held Avery on the other side of the elevator. "You're such an asshole!"

"I knew," Jasmine spoke up. "It was the first high school party I went to. Then I was offered to tutor Stuart. He was the only person left seeking tutoring." A look of disgust appeared on her face. "But I was too scared to be alone with him. I almost got kicked from the program until you requested to be tutored. I'm scared of him and I promised myself I'd never be scared of a man but I couldn't keep my promise. I wrote him down on the list."

"That's not true," Bleu said shakily.

"It is true." Her hands shook as she handed the notebook off to Bleu.

Bleu snatched her marble notebook, read it and threw it back over at her. She folded her arms and leaned in the corner with a distressed look on her burning red face.

"I didn't really know who you were. I didn't know your name, Bleu, I just knew your face. But I used to pray for you, all the time."

An untamed tear rolled down Bleu's cheek. After the passing minutes of everyone reflecting on what just happened, Bleu spoke up. "I'm sorry, Mercury."

Soon enough, it was five in the afternoon in the elevator. Jasmine, Avery and Eden fell asleep most likely in the hopes they'd wake up and this would all be over. I had tried to get some rest myself until Bleu and Quincy began talking to one another. I squinted my eyes so I could see the scene.

"What happened to your eye?" Quincy asked.

Bleu laughed and shifted on to her other foot, she wiped under her nose sniffling.

"What?" Quincy said.

"How did you know?"

"Please," Quincy said. "The sunglasses are a cliche way to cover a black eye."

Bleu bit her lip smiling and took off her sunglasses revealing a pink and purple mixed bruise surrounding her eye. "Well no one has asked me all day."

"Really?"

Bleu nodded. "Yes. It was my father. He found a condom in my room. I talked back and he slapped me so hard, I fell into a block of wood sticking out from my bed. I was bleeding like crazy."

Quincy's eyes roamed her face. "Are you lying to me?" Quincy whispered.

Bleu looked over at her and scoffed before looking at the wall. "I don't lie to you," she said quietly. "I was just as surprised as you were. Did you know?"

"No. No I didn't. Jesus and she's my friend."

I began to wonder if the other girls were pretending to be asleep and were hearing this. "I don't sleep with Stuart. It was my brother, Tom's."

Quincy squinted. "Why didn't you tell your dad that?"

Bleu shrugged. "I told him 'Tom does it'," she laughed. "He said Tom's a boy. It's different with boys'."

Quincy was quiet for a moment. "Does Eden know about your eye?"

"Yeah she asked me if the sex was worth it."

Quincy smiled.

"I said yes," her face contorted into one filled with sorrow. "I'm a horrible sister."

"Nah."

"God, I've been nothing but an asshole to Mercury because I've been so jealous. It's like everytime I try to talk to her: Mercury. Mercury, Mercury, mercury all the time."

Quincy laughed. "Mercury's nice."

"Too nice. She was too nice before the incident. She was great."

Sixteen

I cross out words so you will see them more; the fact that they are obscured makes you want to read them.

• **Jean-Michel Basquiat**

I watched as Avery gradually woke up. Her hair was tousled wildly like falling autumn leaves. She took in her surroundings. "Hey. What time is it?"

I showed her the time on my phone. It was seven.

"Jesus H," she giggled. "Is it weird that I don't mind that this is happening? This is kind of exciting. I mean, I don't want to jinx anything but thank God the light is still on and this elevator is so big. And like there's no telling what's gonna happen next." Avery looked down at my lap. "What are you eating?"

I glanced down at the protein bar I had leftover from lunch.

"I love that stuff."

I took another bite.

"You know protein bars are an aphrodisiac."

I stopped chewing and jerked my head up at her.

Avery snorted. "I'm just kidding. Eat your food." She grabbed her phone off the floor to tend to it.

I smiled, furrowing my eyebrows at the randomness. I continued to eat but as soon as I finished Avery dived to me and pulled me on top of her. My eyes popped out of my head. Avery covered my mouth with her hand and put a finger to her lips. I nodded. She looked back over at Bleu who was rustling in her sleep and then back at me. "Please."

I nodded again with fervor feeling dumbstruck for the millionth time as I always am around her. Avery pressed her plump cherry lips roughly to mine and wrapped her arms around me. I was in heaven. My pink hair encompassed her like a tent. I gently pressed kisses to her lips, to her chin and descending down her chest. Avery started giggling. I reattached my lips to hers and kissed her more hungrily. I bit her swollen lip and a single moan escaped her mouth. Suddenly, Bleu began to mumble in her sleep. I rapidly shifted to the corner of the elevator.

Avery, breathing heavily, erupted into giggles. She was completely disheveled and it gave me a sense of power. I silenced the loudest person. I gave out a nervous laugh. She crawled over to me in a seductive yet amusing fashion and began to kiss me recklessly open mouthed. I don't know what came over me. Maybe it was how delicately her red hair fell lightly over her eyes or the way her smile faded into a passionate look of adoration whenever she pressed her lips against me, but something about her made me leave my eyes open when I kissed her back. Her eyelashes fluttered against my cheek. She blinked her eyes open. She slowly moved off of me. Brown eyes mixed with green like the Earth's ground and dewy grass.

"You're really into me, huh?" she asked. I gulped. My

face grew red with embarrassment. A smile was spread smooth like butter across her face.

Eden rubbed at her eyes making Avery stand up abruptly. "Good morning, sunshine!" Avery exclaimed.

Jasmine narrowed her eyes as she woke up squinting from the light. "What time is it?"

"Seven."

"Seven?!" Bleu exclaimed. She pulled her phone out of her pocket and checked it. "Ugh!"

"Hey listen, Bleu. I'm sorry if what I said earlier offended you. I was just mad."

Bleu sat up. She pressed down her golden blonde curls. "Um no I'm sorry, too-."

"No," Avery interrupted. "You were right. I did sleep around and took a lot of drugs. I'll put it all out on the table. Mostly amphetamine. It was pathetic." Avery chuckled. She plopped back down next to me.

"It's okay," Bleu said. "It's none of my business."

Everyone was awake at 7:45. Bleu pulled out a large Five Star red notebook and began drawing with a ballpoint pen. I crawled across the elevator and looked at her drawing curiously. I watched as Eden's face started to appear in advanced jerky sketches. I smiled in amazement.

"Pretty good, huh?" Bleu asked.

I nodded.

"Let's play I have never," Avery blurted out. She was holding a silver coated hip flask. She let it rock back and forth between two of her fingers.

"What's that?

"A drinking game."

"I don't drink," Jasmine stared matter-of-factly.

"Me neither," Eden said.

"You don't have to play if you don't want to. None of you do."

"I do," Bleu said.

"How do you play?" Jasmine asked.

"Someone says they have never done something and whoever has, drinks."

"Sounds easy enough," Quincy said.

"I'll start." Avery cleared her throat. "I have never kissed a girl."

I laughed. Then Quincy laughed. She looked at all of us radiating with glee. "Ho ho ho," she clapped her hands together. "Give me." She took a swig from the flask. A disgusted look was displayed across her face. "Ugh."

Everyone laughed. I took the bottle and took a drink, raising my eyebrows at Quincy.

Quincy eyes widened. "Well well well. Hey, Eden take a sip."

Eden snickered. "Very funny."

I gave the bottle back to Avery who was already subtly glaring at me. Avery handed the bottle over to Bleu. Quincy and I waited for Bleu to take a sip but nothing. Her eyes were arrows missing their targets as she peered away from us.

"Um I have never...I don't know jumped off a bridge."

Quincy smiled and took the bottle. "My brother and I were running from Steven and he was catching up too fast."

"Who's Steven?" Jasmine asked.

"My mom's boyfriend at the time. He used to-," Quincy smiled. "No one else has jumped off a bridge?"

"Nah," said Avery.

121

Eden took the bottle. "I have never taken a shit in a port-a-potty."

Avery snorted. "What?" Everyone drank from the flask.

Jasmine said, "I have never smoked weed."

Bleu drank while staring at Quincy.

Quincy drank, too. In fact, they all took a sip except for me.

"I have never been to Paris," Quincy stated. A smile that was once there was gone.

Bleu sipped from the flask.

"I have never had a near death experience," Avery said.

Quincy drank and I did, too.

"I have never been to jail," Bleu said.

Quincy took a small sip staring into space.

"I have never gotten a tattoo," Eden said her eyes were on Quincy now. Quincy took a drink and Avery did as well.

"Uh." Jasmine tried not to look at Quincy. "I've never had sex in the back of a car."

Avery took a sip with Quincy.

"Never had a pet," Quincy said quietly.

Everyone drinks.

"I have never been shot at," said Avery.

Quincy drinks.

"I have never watched someone die in front of me," Avery spoke again.

Quincy took a drink hesitantly.

"I have never seen someone shot at in real life." Avery wouldn't stop but no one stopped her.

Quincy goes to take a drink but her fist clenches up.

I looked over at Bleu who's also nervously looking at Quincy and shook my head.

"I don't think we should play anymore," Bleu blurted out.

"Why?" Avery asked. "We have to play until the bottle finishes."

Quincy covered her face and screamed into her hands insanely loud making everyone jump.

Bleu got up and threw the bottle from Quincy over to Avery. "I said I don't think we should play anymore!"

Quincy stood up shaking. She was crying hysterically. "He was on the bridge I sh-should've pushed him off. I should've pushed him off with me and looked behind me! He was right behind me. I should've known he wouldn't jump off. He didn't have to fucking shoot him!" She gripped her head. She was jumping up and down in the elevator the tears racing down her face. She fell to the floor with her hair balled in her fists. "He didn't have to shoot him because he didn't want to drown and he made him drown in blood. He kept coughing it up and his eyes were so white." She was crying so much. My stomach clenched with guilt.

Jasmine, startled, went translucently pale. She looked at the rest of us in shock.

Quincy was breathing heavier than normal. "He didn't have t-to shoot him like that." Her cries became mixed with sharp coughs. Bleu wrapped her arms around her shoulders, shushing her. She brought the two of them back against the wall. She looked over at me and mimicked using an inhaler.

My hands were shaking. I went into Quincy's bag and through the pockets sure enough there was an inhaler. I handed it to Bleu.

Bleu put it into Quincy's mouth.

"In his belly. He didn't have to throw him so hard." She shook her head violently gasping for air.

Bleu nodded and pushed the inhaler into her mouth.

Quincy took it and used it. She deflated like a balloon. I sat back down. I was so overwhelmed, I almost started crying again.

"What were you trying to do?!" Bleu shouted at Avery.

"I-I thought she was bluffing to get more sips in."

I pushed Quincy's hair off her face as her eyes started closing.

"Why did you go to jail?" Avery asked.

"Stop!" Bleu yelled.

"I wanna know. Don't you?"

"No?!"

"To visit my mom," Quincy said innocently.

"No more questions," Bleu said instantly. "Don't ask her anything."

Eden walked beside me without a care in the world. I could tell because she was wearing sunglasses and it was already 6:00 at night. "If you were a cartoon character, who would you be?" she asked me out of the blue.

"Hmmm..." I bit my lip. "Probably Squidward."

"Aw man I knew you were gonna say a character from SpongeBob. God, you're so predictable, it's like you don't even try."

"No but c'mon I'm Squidward."

"He's constantly bitter."

"So am I!"

"Oh god." She instantly stopped walking.

"What?" I asked.

"It's the nymphomaniac."

I looked in her direction and noticed a familiar brunette

talking to two guys on the bench on the boardwalk. "Oh her? Leave her alone, Eden."

"Why? She is."

"It's not a reason to hate her."

"Did I say I hate her?"

I folded my arms across my chest. "I'd be a fool to think you didn't," *I replied.*

Eden stared at her for awhile. She pushed her sunglasses up on her head. "She's... too much."

"Too much," *I said trying to comprehend it.* "Not much but too much."

"Exactly. It's like she can't be nice to you she has to be extra nice to you."

I couldn't take it anymore and sputtered out a laugh. "Are you out of your mind?"

"She's too dramatic. That's hysterical not me."

"I like her." *I gulped.* "She seems nice."

Eden snorted. We continued our stride again. "Why?" *She asked.* "Do you even talk to her?"

I thought about it for a second. We had a conversation in middle school last year about frogs. She kept making a cute face whenever she said "ewwww". *Not cute but, I don't know.* "Sure I do."

"When? I don't believe you. You're always hanging out with me."

"Whenever I'm not...that's when I'm with her."

Eden stopped walking again and pointed towards her. "I dare you to go up to her right now and have a conversation."

I purposely flared open my nostrils. "Fine I will. When she's finished." *Almost on cue the two guys previously by her side, get up to leave and wave to her. She waved back flirtatiously.*

"Now's your chance," Eden said.

I rolled me eyes. "Fine." I walked over to her, feeling each board crack as I did so. I reluctantly sat beside her without saying a word.

Avery turned to face me with a frown. "Mercury?

"Sup, Avery." I leaned back coyly and knocked over a water bottle that was balancing on the back of the bench. "Shit, sorry."

"It's fine it wasn't mine."

"Oh okay." I folded my sweaty hands in my lap.

"How are you?"

That's a good way to start this up. "I'm good...good. And you?"

Avery shrugged and cocked her head. "Eh. I'm here."

That made me smile. "Me, too."

"What do you do now?" she asked.

"Sorry?"

"Like what has changed in your life?"

"Nothing. It's pathetic."

Avery grinned and shook her head. "I'm sorry, I'm like so high right now." I studied her round glossy eyes. Her possessor blocking me from the real Mercury. I waved it off but I couldn't help but be upset about it.

"That's okay."

Avery bit her lip. "It's not okay. I've been wondering and preparing for when we'd be able to talk again." She laughed. "And now I'm high."

"That's alright. Just enjoy it."

She facepalmed herself. "I'm sorry. I'm so stupid." One of the boys that was sitting next to Avery before came back over with popcorn. He gave a small smile to me before he took a seat next to her. "I'm gonna go," I said innocently.

"I'm sorry."

I nodded and threw a peace sign and headed back over to Eden on the bench in front of the funnel cake stand. Eden was smirking. Her elbows resting behind her and her legs crossed.

"Well well you did it. What'd you two chat about?"

"Nothing."

"Well you had to have conversed about something. Your lips were moving."

"We didn't talk about anything important." I shook my head. "She's high."

Eden laughed and instantaneously covered her mouth.

"It's not funny, Eden."

She held her hands up in surrender. "Why the aggressiveness?"

"I don't know," I said aggressively.

Eden stopped laughing and rubbed my shoulder. "That is kind of disappointing."

I nodded.

"It's whatever. Want some ice cream? I'll go get some. Mint chocolate?" Eden asked rising off the bench.

"Uh..."

"Mint chocolate it is."

I watched Avery and the boy get up to leave across the boardwalk. I noticed a bright lime green headband left behind on it. I retrieved the headband and ran after her. After dodging a few couples, I was able to catch up to her completely out of breath. "Avery," I made out.

Avery turned around confused with the boy. "Mercury?" She smiled. "Hi again."

"Hi again. You um...you left your headband."

"That's not mine. You can go ahead, Mike."

Mike walked ahead.

"It's not yours?"

Avery shook her head.

"Oh." I nodded still out of breath.

Avery was still gleaming.

"I really like...like..." Avery blinked. "Mmm," I laughed awkwardly at a loss for words. I placed my hands on my hips. "Your hair."

"Thanks." She ran her hand back through it. "I was actually about to dye it."

"Really? What color?"

"Blue. Like a baby blue, you know?"

I laughed. "Oh I thought you were gonna say red."

"Why, red?"

I remember you said it was your favorite color, I thought to myself. "I don't know you just seem like you can pull off being a redhead. They're fiery."

She smiled coyly. "I told you my favorite color is red." She raised an eyebrow. "Remember?"

"Oh yeah." I looked away from her and cleared my throat.

Avery's smile faded. She lowered her voice and said, "You know you're really fucking cute."

My knees got weak. My cheeks grew hot with a feeling I couldn't identify. Avery sputtered into a laugh. "Bye, Mercury." She jogged over to Mike who was walking away slow enough for her to catch up. Amiable Avery.

-

I knocked vehemently on Eden's window. Eden opened it with a confused tired look on her face. "Can you dye my hair?" I asked.

"You want to dye your hair? She processed slowly.

"Yeah."

128

"Why...?"

"'Cause."

"What color?

"Pink."

Eden rubbed her eyes sleepily trying to focus on me. "Are you being forreal?"

"Yeah."

She sighed. "Alright, Frenchy." She laughed at her Grease reference amid me rolling my eyes. "You'll have to ask Bleu. I don't know how to dye." She made me scrunch my face up into disgust.

"Bleu?"

Eden shrugged. It was my turn to sigh. Eden helped me in and led me over to Bleu's room. Her light was still on which meant she wasn't asleep. Eden opened the door. When she spotted us, Bleu took off her headphones. "I told you to knock."

"Knock," Eden said apathetically. "Mercury wants to ask you something."

Bleu discreetly rolled her eyes. She swung her legs over the edge of the bed to face the two of us. "Hi, Bleu," I said and cleared my throat. "I was wondering if you could dye my hair maybe. If you're not busy."

"I'm always busy," she spoke immediately.

"Oh," I said.

"Don't be a bitch," Eden said. "She's my only friend that indubitably tolerates you for reasons I can't decipher."

Bleu laughed at that statement. "She's your only friend."

"Will you do it or not?" Eden asked.

I gave a small friendly smile and wiped it off my face when she didn't return the gesture.

Bleu and I went to Walmart the next day looking for the dye. I began wondering if Avery actually dyed her hair red. Even if she did, she would have done it because it's her favorite color. Not because I asked her to. What would she think if I dyed my hair pink? Oh my god she's going to laugh at me. Not just any laugh. I'm talking about some serious cackling

"Mercury?" Bleu called sternly. My attention snapped to Bleu standing in front of boxes of hair dye. The distinct sound of people checking out items at the cash register flooded into my ears. "What color? I asked you like ten times."

"Oh uh pink."

"What?"

"Pink."

Bleu bit her lip so she wouldn't laugh.

"Not even gonna ask." She took it off the shelf.

"If people laugh, I'll say you did it."

Bleu's eyes widened. "You wouldn't."

"Watch me."

"Are you trying to impress somebody?" Bleu asked inquisitively.

I scoffed. "What?"

Bleu smirked. "Yeah you like somebody."

"Everyone likes somebody."

Bleu bit her lip and nodded. "I'll figure it out."

I scoffed. "You won't. Trust me."

-

"No skateboarding in the halls," a teacher said. I looked over at the elderly woman glaring at me. I angrily picked up my board and accidentally knocked shoulders with somebody. "Oh sorry." I turned my head and faced Avery. Fuck.

Her hair was bright red.

Avery gasped. "This. Is. Sick!" Avery held my pink hair in my hands. Meanwhile, my hands were shaking like crazy. "I never thought I'd say this but pink is definitely your color."

"Th-thanks."

Bleu hastily walked up to Avery and I with Rachel. She removed Avery's hands off my hair. Avery glanced back and forth between the two of us with confusion written all over her face. Bleu smoothed my hair down. "This took almost two hours to do. Don't mess it up."

"Sorry." Avery laughed. "I don't see what damage I could have possibly provoked."

"Just don't touch it. Alright?" Bleu narrowed her eyes. "Can you handle that?"

Rachel laughed.

Avery snarled at her. "Alright, mija, relax." She looked her over.

Bleu rolled her eyes and walked off with Rachel.

"Wow. Nice novia, Mercury."

"She isn't my girlfriend," I said defensively and a tad too quickly.

Avery smiled. "I was just kidding."

"I know." I glanced around before awkwardly placing my skateboard back on the ground. Always trying to find a way to embarrass myself, aren't I?

Avery scratched the top of her head. "I didn't know you two were like...friends."

"We're not." I looked up. "She's just my neighbor."

"She's kind of a bitch."

"Oh yeah yeah. Yeah she can be."

Avery stood quietly analyzing me. "I should start heading home." Avery only stared at me.

I nodded and tried to step past her.

"Wait uh." She tucked her hands into her scarlet jacket pockets. "I'm sorry about the other day."

"Don't worry about it-"

"One of my guy friends offered me something to drink and I didn't know it had shit in it so..."

"I said not to worry about it," I emphasized.

"Well I'm gonna worry about it," she said. "If you want to pick a phrase to move past this conversation, just say it's okay."

I clenched my fists. "It's okay."

"Okay." She rolled her eyes. "You can go now."

I scoffed. "Fine." I hopped on my skateboard.

"Fine. Tell Bleu I said hi."

"I'm sure she would love to hear from you!" I called from down the hall.

"I didn't think you'd end up being a bitch, Mercury!"

"Neither did I!" I opened the school doors and left kind of amused.

-

Couples were making out intensely on the stairwell. All the single boys were crowding around a beer keg in the kitchen. Typical party. Feeling a little overwhelmed, I headed for the front door to exit but there she stood. She was leaning against the speakers blasting catchy modern pop songs. Avery rolled her eyes at me and took a sip of her drink. I walked over to her without remembering that I did. "Sorry," I blurted out.

"Sorry for what?" She asked not looking at me.

"I can't remember," I breathed out.

Avery smiled to herself.

"You look really nice," I said.

"Thanks," she said emotionlessly. She viewed the party scene

avoiding my gaze. I wallowed in the silence waiting for her to say something.

"Oh thanks!" I exclaimed out of the blue. "Yeah, I like this outfit, too."

Avery doubled over laughing.

"I curled my hair myself," I continued. "Eden did my makeup. First house party, so I tried to look my best."

Avery caught her breath and rested a hand on my shoulder. She looked at my outfit. "You look like a lesbian."

I held my breath. "Really?"

Avery shook her head. "No. I'm sure I do, though."

I laughed. "You don't."

"No?" She glanced back up and nodded in agreement with me. Her hand was still on my shoulder. I looked at it and she noticed. A small smile formed on her lips.

"My head is pounding from this music," I said.

"Yeah I hate it, too."

"And this soda tastes like medicine."

"Totally tastes like medicine," she set it down. I spotted that irritating kid, Stuart, staring at me from across the room. He's always trying to be the class clown in Ceramics. "I totally saw him staring at you, too."

I laughed turning pink in the face. "He's not attractive to me."

"What? Are you blind?"

I smiled. "Must be."

"You know this is my house?"

I screamed internally. Of course it is! "Really?"

"Uh huh." She tapped her thumb against my neck. "Yeah you like it now?"

"It's a nice home."

Avery finally removed her hand. She stood closer to me. "Are you going to the next house party? It's at Stuart's." She took another sip.

"Maybe."

A kid saddled up to Avery. He wrapped an arm around her shoulders.

I looked down at my feet.

"I'm busy here." She tried pushing him away. The guy smiled and whispered in her ear making her smile. I walked out of the house without saying a word. I don't know what I was doing there anyway.

"Hey, Mercury wait."

"Nah I'm gonna go home," I called back.

"Mercury?"

I sighed and stopped walking. I turned around to look up at her standing on the step. "What?"

She slowly began to smile. She shook her head. "Don't ever give up on me like that again."

Seventeen

When it comes down to it, I let people think what they want. And if they care enough to bother with what I do, I already know I'm better than them.

- Marilyn Monroe

Avery was on her phone playing a game. "Don't you think you should save your battery life?" Bleu asked. Avery glared at her. Bleu shook her head, smiling. "Fine."

Quincy was fast asleep again. "How'd you know about the inhaler?" Jasmine asked Bleu.

"I'm observant." Bleu reached into her book bag and pulled out a pack of Marlboros. "Anyone have a lighter?"

"I just think it's funny that you wanted to know so much about Mercury's traumatic past but not Quincy's."

"Yeah." Eden laughed. She sat up taller. "I almost missed that."

"That is a very valid point," Avery said rubbing her chin.

"I don't know what you're implying," Bleu said laughing. "But whatever you're implying is fallacious."

"Fallacious, is it?" Avery asked.

"Yeah. It is." Bleu tightened her grip around Quincy.

"I'm not used to seeing people like that. First Mercury, now apathetic Quincy of all people. I just...it's been a weird trip in here. Who's next? Me? I don't have anything that big to hide but I'm afraid I do."

"I'm seeing Jack Silverstein." Jasmine said with a pained look on her face. Avery stood up off the ground.

"What?!" Avery exclaimed. I gave her a look filled with confusion.

"Please don't tell me he's problematic," Jasmine said.

"Absolutely. He's the only guy that passed up sleeping with me."

Eden giggled to herself and I rolled my eyes.

"It's not funny," Avery pointed out.

"Well it's fine by me. Anyway, my parents would kill me if they found out I had a boyfriend. No one in my family has had romantic relations with a white person. They don't like change. I tried to leave the house without my hijab once." She pointed to her garments. "And surprisingly my mom was the one who lost her shit. Not my dad." Avery tried to subtly cover up her exposed chest with her arms.

When she finished speaking all of us turned to face Eden. "I don't feel like sharing," Eden mumbled ignoring my gaze.

Then everyone looked at Bleu. "I don't have anything really."

"You don't have to share," Eden said.

"There's nothing to share." Everyone continued to stare at her.

Avery just sighed. "If she doesn't want to share, she doesn't share." She put her headphones back on.

Bleu blinked and stared at her feet biting her lip. "Fine…" Her eyes roamed at all of the girls faces. Her boldness dissipated and she analyzed her fingers so she wouldn't have to look at all of us. "Quincy left her cleats in her locker and I left my bag in the locker room. This was yesterday," she clarified. "So we asked the janitor to unlock the locker room for us at 8pm. I was feeling antsy about the game which is tonight so I made her practice with me. Then it started raining but I hadn't notice until I slipped in the grass and landed on Quincy's leg, as she was trying to kick the ball from between mine. I tried to get up but I kept slipping. When I finally stood up, my cleats gave out again and I landed back on Quincy. My lips landed on hers. It was an accident. Happy?"

So she kissed her again. Eden gasped.

"What happened after you kissed her on the field?" Jasmine asked.

"I don't remember."

"Sure you do," Avery looked at me as she spoke. "You kissed a girl, you have to remember the whole thing."

"It wasn't a kiss. We didn't kiss. It was an accident."

"Yeah you did," Eden said. "You took psychology. Remember Freud? There are no accidents." I laughed.

Bleu shook her head. "I'm not gay."

"We're not saying you are," Avery said condescendingly. "We're just inferring that you may have feelings for Quincy."

"My mistake," Bleu said.

"What happened after the kiss?" Jasmine asked again intrigued.

"I grabbed my ball and my bag and ran home before she could get up."

"Why'd you run away?" Jasmine pressed.

"I didn't run away," Bleu said defensively. "I just ran home that's all."

"So you guys haven't talked about it?"

"No it was an accident."

Everyone except me said in unison. "There are no accidents."

Quincy began to rustle in her sleep.

"I have an idea," Eden spoke up. "We're all gonna pretend we're asleep to give you two privacy."

"We are?" Avery asked.

"Yes, we are."

"But it wouldn't be private if you guys can hear what's happening."

Quincy stirred awake.

Everyone closed their eyes. I squinted mine open again.

Bleu quickly removed her hands off of Quincy. "Hey."

"Hi." She stood up to stretch. "Wow everyone's knocked out."

"Yeah," Bleu said. "Weird."

"Did you get any sleep?" She sat down against the metallic door.

"Wha-yes. Yes I did."

"What about yesterday?"

"Yesterday? Maybe. Or maybe not because I have insomnia."

"Oh okay." She wiped her eyes, yawning.

They were dead silent. Imagine not being able to escape an awkward situation. There was nothing to look at, nowhere to go and nothing else to do. Quincy started whistling. She drummed her lap with her hands as she did so. Bleu coughed and said, "I'm sorry about falling on you."

"It's cool."

Bleu nodded unsure of what to do with her hands.

"How's your legs?" Quincy's eyes widened. "From the fall," she corrected hastily.

"They're fine," Bleu said. "How's yours considering I fell on them?"

"They're a-ok."

"That's good." Silence was trapped in the elevator again. Heat rose up to her cheeks.

"It's okay if you fall on me again by accident or something."

"Right," Bleu said.

"That was weird." Quincy blinked. "I meant like during the game, if you fell on me, I wouldn't be mad."

Bleu nodded. "Okay."

Quincy laughed at herself, shaking her head and looked at her phone as a distraction. "That whole freak out, that was embarrassing."

"No. I'm sorry you lost someone."

"Shit happens. It was a long time ago. I guess being in such a small space this long is messing with my emotions. I'll be fine. Thank you, though." She held up the inhaler. "For this."

"Yeah. No problem."

"It's empty now so no more freak outs." Quincy held her knees to her chest and then flicked her eyes upward towards Bleu. She rolled her eyes and snorted. "You look at everyone like that?"

I caught Jasmine squinting her eyes.

"Like what?"

"You're always looking at me like I twisted my ankle."

"What?" Bleu laughed.

"I can't explain it. You know the face someone makes when they say 'aww poor thing'."

Bleu snickered. "I'm sorry. I'm nervous that we won't make it out of here."

"I can tell. You keep apologizing." Quincy moved to sit next to Bleu. "You know what I do when I'm nervous?"

"What?"

"I scream."

"I'm not screaming."

Quincy covered her ears with a grin. "Do it."

"I'm not screaming. They're asleep."

"Then whisper scream like this," she cupped her hands around her mouth and put it to Bleu's ear. "Hahhhhh!"

Bleu began giggling. "No."

"C'mon."

Bleu stared at her with longing. "I don't think I'm nervous anymore," she said quietly.

Quincy stared back at her in silence. "I was asking my mom--the last day I saw her before she went to jail--where she was going and she wasn't answering me. I was seven." Bleu nodded for her to continue. "She was stuffing things into her bag. Lots of food and stuff while my little brother was crying. Then she fled out of the house. She didn't lock the door behind her."

"So I had to make dinner. Our microwave wasn't working and the lights were shut off by the superintendent. It was pitch black. Steven wanted dinner, too, once he came home, and I didn't have enough for three so he got angry. We went to get fast food but he was drunk so I had to help him with the wheel. He didn't buy us anything to eat. Eventually, my mom called him and told him everything but Steven didn't want to take care of us. I remember he flashed his grill, growling at me and gripped me with his arm. I was paralyzed by his anger. With his other hand, he reached for the glove compartment. My little brother and I started taking off out of the car because we were stuck in traffic. The sky was purple and I couldn't breathe by the cold mixed with the smog and I felt like I was drowning before Steven caught up to us with the gun in his hands. I had to jump off the bridge into the water."

"I was telling my brother to jump but I knew he was dead. He had a geyser of blood erupting from his mouth. His eyes were cloud white. It was like there was no blood in them. He was alive during the whole thing." Quincy shook her head crying. "I should have pushed him off before I jumped." She let out a shaky breath. "I was nervous so I screamed."

Bleu gave a pathetic scream. "There don't tell anyone I did that."

Quincy wiped her eyes and laughed. "Do you think we're winning the game right now?"

"The three best players are in this elevator. What do you think?"

"I think anything is possible. Anything."

"Me, too." Bleu swallowed as she stared at Quincy.

"I'm sorry for kissing you," Quincy blurted out. "The first time. I didn't think I'd embarrass you so much."

Bleu stared at her hands. She selected a cigarette out of the box.

"You're gonna smoke in here?" Quincy asked. Bleu took her lighter out. "I read somewhere that you shouldn't do that in an elevator," Quincy said.

The lighter wouldn't ignite. "Damn it."

Quincy watched her.

Bleu pointed at her. "Shut up, Quincy."

"I didn't say anything."

Bleu kicked Avery in the shin. Avery pretended to wake up. It was the most unbelievable acting I've ever witnessed. "Oh, cut the crap. I need a lighter."

Avery reached into the front pocket of her bag and pulled out a yellow lighter. "How did you know I had one?"

Bleu lit her cigarette and took a drag. She breathed it out relieved.

Eighteen

In three words I can sum up everything I've learned about life: it goes on.

- **Robert Frost**

Words are so funny. They could be so powerful. Someone can say a phrase during a certain situation and have it mean absolutely nothing. Someone else can say the same phrase and make it mean everything. Like saying 'I need to pee' when you're at your house and you have to excuse yourself from your guests. But when you're in a large yet compact elevator comprised of five other girls, the phrase is practically life changing.

"I need to pee," Jasmine said. All the girls looked at her with scared looks in their eyes.

"Me, too," Eden said.

"Y'all can't pee in here," Avery said. "That's just crazy."

"We can use like a container or something."

"We don't have dicks! You can't piss in a container!"

"I don't think I can hold it."

"That's it," Quincy stood up. "I saw this in the movies once. Mercury get over here."

Confused, I stood up.

"Lift me up I wanna see if I can get this shaft open."

I looked up. "Andale."

I grabbed her up by her legs and lifted her up off the ground.

She banged her fists roughly against the ceiling tile and sure enough it opened. "Oh thank God." She pushed it across the top of it. "Ugh it's humid as hell in here." She lifted herself up with her hands.

Bleu stood up and stood by me. She peered up at Quincy. "What do you see?" she asked.

"Walls. But some space between the elevator and the walls. Wow we're actually high up. Really high."

"Anywhere to go."

"No. Oh you mean use the bathroom? Well there's these spaces. It's pretty dark in here so I don't think anyone goes down there."

"Help me up, Mercury," Eden said next.

I lifted her up with Quincy's assistance and then I lifted Jasmine. Eden took off her pants and went near the edge.

"Wait. We can't have you falling." Quincy kneeled and held her hand.

"Thanks." She said when she finished. "This is probably the weirdest place I can say I have ever, you know, *went* in."

"A'ight get down. Enough of you."

Eden jumped down and into the elevator contently.

Quincy turned around and glanced at Jasmine. "Jas, you can go with that on?"

"Yes, I can," she spoke firmly in irritation. "I've done this before."

Quincy raised her hands above her head. "Alright."

Jasmine lifted the dress up and sat down but she was sitting on it. She bundled up the fabric from underneath her and scooted closer to the edge. Parts of the dress in the front kept falling in front of her. "Jesus." Jasmine abruptly slips on the corner. I gasped.

"Woah!" Quincy caught her by her waist in the nick of time.

"What's going on?" Avery asked worriedly.

"I'll take it off," Jasmine said.

"Good," Quincy said wiping her brow.

Jasmine rose up and attempted taking it off but the hijab nearly gets taken off with it. "Whoops." She tries again and the same thing happened.

"Jasmine," Quincy said. Jasmine tried taking it off again with her hand on her head. "Jasmine, you have to- Jasmine?" Jasmine was panting now, going at it again but the hijab begins falling off. "Honey, you have to take it off."

"No. This has never happened before. It's two pieces. It's not supposed to move." Quincy gazed at her worriedly. She scratched her head nervously. Jasmine placed her hands on her hips. A stress filled expression was written all over her face. Jasmine wiped fresh tears from her eyes.

"What are you so afraid of?" Quincy whispered softly for only her to hear. "I thought you didn't want to wear it at one point."

"No one has seen me without it on," Jasmine whispered back.

"No one's gonna judge you, Jas. I'll beat them up if they do. I promise. I could never hesitate to beat someone up."

She nodded. She quickly took her clothes off and threw them on the floor. A silky black bun was revealed. She went over to the edge of the elevator. I watched as Quincy held her hand and closed her eyes. Jasmine was complaining crestfallen.

Quincy opened her eyes and stood up. She helped Jasmine off the floor and handed her the garments. "I'm sorry."

Jasmine ignored her and retrieved her clothes. She quickly put them on with a scared look in her eye. Her breathing heightened each time she couldn't fix the clothes over her head right away.

Quincy jumped down and looked to her left. "What happens in this elevator," she looked to her right side. "Stays in this elevator." She helped Jasmine down.

Everyone nodded. I peered over at Jasmine in the corner who still had jet black strands poking out of her hijab. Jasmine was staring at her fingers.

"You have beautiful hair," Avery said.

"Don't. Please," Jasmine said softly. "Thank you but don't."

"Too soon?" Avery asked.

She nodded.

"Since whatever happens in here stays in here," Eden said. "I have a girl crush on you."

Everyone giggled.

Jasmine opened her mouth to speak but nothing came out.

"So does Mercury." Avery tucked her lips in, attempting not to smile. I punched her in the arm as everyone was laughing.

-

The lights in the elevator flickered for a brief moment until almost instantly they shut off. All the girls cried for the first time if they hadn't done so already. Except for Avery and I. Avery instantly attached her lips to mine the second the lights went off. We wrestled like tigers in the dark. Colors bursted behind my eyes like fireworks. All I could see were checkered black and white squares spinning hypnotically. A cornucopia of reds and purples reverberated beneath my eyelids like a psychedelic cyclone. It's amazing how something so beautiful could be neutrally staring at you from across the room one minute and then on top of you in an amorous mess the next. We never got caught. Even when Bleu began using her phone as a flashlight. I honestly think Avery did this to me so I wouldn't be scared.

"My lab partner asked me today what my problem was." It was ten o'clock now. The lights were back on, flickering but not enough to provoke a seizure. Avery looked at all of us. "I know she was obviously trying to be rude but I thought about it. I binge when I'm upset. And I like attention, that's my problem."

"My problem is I can't defend myself," Jasmine admitted. "I welcome things that hurt me."

"My problem is that I miss my mom," Quincy said.

Eden shook her head. "I don't have a problem."

"You love your sister but since she's an asshole to everyone but you," Avery said. "You feel the need to push her away."

Oh boy.

"You don't know me." Eden said instantly.

Bleu sat quietly in the corner staring at the ceiling.

"I don't know if she's an asshole to you," Avery said. "But Mercury does. You shouldn't give a shit about what other people think of Bleu. You shouldn't care because she's your sister and she adores you. Deep down, you know she's not that bad 'cause you know her better than anyone else."

Eden clapped her hands together. "Wow. That was lovely. So, what, you two are best friends now?" She said looking between the two of us. Avery looked as though she was about to burst.

"You really don't get it do you?" Avery scoffed. "I'm not trying to take your place. I didn't swoop in like a demon from the fiery pits of hell and try to steal your best friend away from you on some strange impulse."

"Then what are you doing, exactly?"

"Nothing."

It was Eden's turn to be derisive. "I don't believe that."

Avery smirked to herself. "Neither do I. Just know I'm not trying to take your friend, okay?"

"No. It's not okay."

"You're really stubborn," Jasmine acknowledged.

"Does it look like I care?" Eden asked.

"No but that's because you're stubborn."

Eden's bouncy curly hair shook every time she moved around. "If some random chick started taking your friend everywhere and you weren't included, wouldn't you be upset?"

Quincy started laughing at Eden with a look of disbelief on her face.

"What?" Eden asked.

Quincy bit her lip. "I mean..." Quincy scratched her head. "I know Avery. I don't mean to put Avery and Mercury on the spot or anything but clearly-"

Avery coughed really loudly.

Eden frowned. "Clearly what?" Quincy looked at Avery while Avery was subtly trying to shake her head.

"Nothing." Quincy bit her tongue.

There was a long awkward silence that followed. Eden looked heartbroken.

Avery rubbed her arms. She had the same discouraged expression on her face from when she looked at herself in the mirror in the dance studio. Without thinking, I leaned over and pressed my lips against Avery's. They were as intensely soft as her demeanor. My eyes were closed but I could feel her lips grow into a beautiful smile. Obscure shapes and colors moved around in my head creating an intense feeling.

"Oh," Eden said.

I moved off with a smile. Avery pretended to faint.

All the girls looked at us with genuine smiles.

"My problem," Bleu said. "Is that I can't admit to things."

Eden was rocking back and forth in the corner of the elevator. Sweat was dripping down her forehead.

"We're never getting out of here," Eden said with her knees tucked into her chest. Bleu tried to calm her down but Eden's aggressive complaints got more intense with every passing second. Eden got up and banged on the doors of the elevator with her fists.

"Eden," Bleu said. Eden tried opening the door with her fingers. "Hey. Eden, come over here."

A whimper escaped Eden's mouth. She gradually pulled out a pocket knife from her maroon jacket pocket. Everyone gasped. I was stuck to the ground frozen like an ice sculpture. My heart was thumping in my ears.

"Woah," Quincy said. She tried slowly slinking away.

"Eden?" Jasmine said in dismay.

Bleu cautiously stood up off the floor. "Eden?"

Eden looked around at all of us with a frightened look in her eye. "No leave me alone. I'm not gonna do anything. I'm not gonna hurt anyone else."

"I believe you," said Bleu. She held her hand out towards Eden. "Give it to me then."

"No." Her chest expanding and deflating as she began to almost hyperventilate. "Go away."

"You're doing really well, Eden. Come on. You don't need to do this now. You don't need to do this again."

She closed her eyes biting her bottom lip. "Yes, I do."

Bleu tried to steal the knife but Eden was stronger. She pulled back roughly and Bleu fell on Quincy.

"I-I have to do this." She hastily rolled her jacket sleeve up. "It makes me forget things."

"Stop, kid," Quincy said while reaching to snatch the knife from her seat. Avery scurried over to the other side of the elevator and tried to take the knife but Eden fought back. In the act she grazed Avery's cheek. Avery felt the cut on her face and looked at the blood on her hands.

I grabbed a packet of tissues from my bag. I rushed over to Avery and frantically pressed the tissue to her cheek streaked with blood. Eden was backing into the corner and gripping the knife. She held it up to her wrist. "Eden, stop!"

Everyone turned to face me.

A smile formed on Avery's face. She punched my arm with her free hand and laughed maniacally. She grabbed my cheeks to press rough kisses to them.

"Mercury, you can talk!" Jasmine exclaimed.

I giggled, "Yeah I guess I can."

"We must have grown on you," Avery said. She winked at me.

"Yeah," I said.

Eden's hands were shaking violently. The knife in her hand fell to the floor. Immediately, she engulfed me in a bear hug and bawled into my neck.

Jasmine hugged us, too. Soon Avery and Quincy joined in. "C'mon Bleu," Quincy said. "Everyone go towards Bleu." We all moved towards Bleu in our packed huddle trying not to fall over. We looked like idiots but we didn't care. Bleu was red in the face with laughter. She hugged us back.

-

"If you were given a billion dollars," Bleu paced the room. "What would be the first thing you do?"

"I'd ask why I was just given a billion dollars," Eden said laying against my shoulder. Her and Avery haven't left my side since I spoke.

"No come on I'm serious."

"I would buy a bunch of strippers." Quincy smiled with her eyes closed.

I snorted.

"Are you serious?" Bleu asked.

"I'm serious. What would you do?" Quincy asked

"Buy a really big house. A mansion. And put the best, the absolute best, of everything in it. Best car, best TV, best bed, best everything." She beamed at the thought.

Avery, who was lounging against my chest, said. "I would buy a beach house."

"You already live by the ocean," I said.

Avery looked back up at me. "But not the beach," she pointed out.

"I think I would buy a bigger house, too," Jasmine said.

"I mean, that is if we're talking about the first thing I would do. I'd probably get a golden retriever to compliment it."

"I'd buy lots of puppies," said Eden. "Puppies everywhere."

Jasmine laughed.

"What about you, Mercury?" Bleu asked.

I looked at all of them looking at me with a smile tugging on their lips. I beamed. "Give it to the poor."

Everyone got quiet. Avery squished my cheeks with her fingers. "You're nice."

Bleu began drawing Quincy, discreetly not caring that my eyes were glued to her creation. She sketched her hair from light to dark. She refused to miss a single detail. She even curved her black Ray Ban eyeglasses the correct way. Quincy realized and tried to keep still when she felt her lightning blue eyes on her. Bleu's eyes pierced into her soul. Bleu released a smile when Quincy started playfully crossing her eyes.

"Has anyone in here thought about just ending it all?" Jasmine asked. "You know, other than the obvious person."

Quincy jumped and looked over at Jasmine as if she did something wrong. "Only all the time."

"I write some ways down," Bleu said. Quincy glanced back at Bleu.

"That's crazy," Jasmine said.

"I only have thirty. It calms me down. I like number 28: laying down in an intersection."

"Have you done that?" asked Quincy.

"No but I want to," Bleu admitted.

Quincy gave a cheeky grin. "That sounds kind of fun."

Jasmine sighed. "You two are a strange pair.".

"There's so many things I wanna do before I die, though," Jasmine said.

"Anything you wanna do?" Eden asked. "Or something you heard you'd enjoy doing? Like skydiving, for example. I hate heights."

"I wanna put my mom in rehab," Avery confessed. "I want her to dance like she did when I was five at the country bar across the street from where my grandma used to live. I don't like heights either. I'm afraid of falling from them and I usually do."

Eden stared at her with an emotion I couldn't pinpoint. It made me wonder if they were ever gonna be friends after this. Quincy said she wanted to go to Paris before she died. It was followed by Bleu declaring it wasn't all that. Pretentiously, I might add, Quincy didn't care. She said she'd bring June and Lily. Jasmine said she wanted to visit there too. Bleu looked over at me when she shared that she would want to do something different with her hair.

"Mercury?"

I glanced up at Jasmine startled. I still wasn't used to being asked my opinion.

"Well?"

"Watch Z get married to William."

"I knew he was gay," Quincy said unfazed.

"Of course you did," Bleu retorted.

Quincy stuck her pink tongue out. "My parents are probably crying looking for me right now."

Suddenly, Jasmine's phone started ringing.

Bleu sat up excitedly.

Jasmine fumbled with her phone and pressed the green lit up button that we couldn't have appreciated more than

Sade Josephine

we did at that moment. She put the call on speaker. "Hello? Hello?!"

"Why the hell haven't you been answering my texts?" A familiar high pitched voice asked irritated. I started laughing and everyone except Jasmine looked at me with confusion.

"Excuse me?" Jasmine said.

"No, you listen to me. I love you a lot okay and I'm worried sick about you. And I just cried okay? And I don't cry. Jas, if you wanted to break up with me, you could have at least said something." The girls cover their mouths to muffle their laughter.

Jasmine tried not to laugh. "Jack, I'm stuck in an elevator!"

Jack became quiet. "Is that code for cheating on me? Or is this relationship an elevator and you feel like you're stuck?"

"Jack I need you to listen to me. I'm at school I'm trapped in an elevator near the auditorium with 5 other girls." She motioned for us to speak. "Say hi."

"Hi, Jack!" Everyone said.

"Holy moly," Jack muttered.

"Jack, you gotta call someone to help us."

"Um okay uh this is a lot of pressure. Where's my phone?"

"Babe, you're on your phone."

"Oh right. Okay I'll try to call you back when I'm done. I'll phone 9-11."

"I owe you one."

"This isn't a prank right?" He asked.

"No! Please. And expect a huge talk when you get me outta here."

Everyone heard him swear under his breath. "Right. Okay. Bye."

"Bye." Jasmine hung up, sighing with relief. She rocked

back and forth grinning. "We're getting out of here." Everyone got quiet. This was actually...fun. I'm sure the other girls were thinking the same thing.

"We should exchange numbers," Quincy said cautiously. "To talk maybe." Bleu looked at Quincy and smiled. We all got each other's phone numbers and reverted back to our positions--spread out on the white tiles. "I don't think any of you will want to chill with me after school tomorrow."

"Not if you say things like 'chill'," Avery said.

Quincy pointed at Avery. "Good point."

"But I will. I definitely will."

"Cool."

"Me, too," Eden said and looked at the both of them with an honest grin.

"Me, three," Jasmine said.

"Me, four," I said.

We all directed our gaze to Bleu impulsively. Except for Quincy. She finally looked up at Bleu and smiled. "It's okay, Bleu."

Bleu gave her that look, again.

Nineteen

"I believe that when we love someone, we respect them, and we listen to them; we feel that their voice matters. And-we let them dictate the terms of who they are and what their story is."

• Laverne Cox

By the time the doors were pried open by a fireman with strange haphazard tattoos all over his arms, I was famished. It was midnight. So many people were staring at us in awe and relief as we were being rescued: police, firemen, the principal and a few other faculty and staff members.

"Hey, ladies," the fireman smiled. Our principal was standing beside him, alongside other firemen, wiping the sweat off his brow. We had to wait by his office to report our names as he informed our parents of our safety. He was thinking two steps ahead because there's no way my dad would have believed I was stuck in an elevator with five other girls for ten hours. I'm not sure I believed it either.

When we got out of the elevator, the girls realized I couldn't talk to the principal. Avery explained the disorder I had to them which made Quincy feel a little ignorant. It was declared that we were excused from school the next day. We didn't know it then but we were all pretty shaken up from that experience.

My dad and I sat in front of Wendy's eating in silence before we headed home. My dad's head rested against the steering wheel. The energy given off was the strongest I've felt from him in a while. He told me he thought he had lost me too.

Before I got home and went to bed, Eden sat on my window sill. One leg in my room and one leg outside.

"I'm sorry that you were assaulted. You should have told me. Wrote me."

I didn't say anything.

"Did you tell your dad? Sylvia?"

I nodded. "Yeah. I have a restraining order against him."

Eden scoffed. "I've been horrible to you because I took your being quiet as ignoring me. It's been a year." Her hands were shaking as she pushed her hair off her face. "I was thinking whatever it was, I knew it was bad. And you still knew I was mad with you even though, I didn't say it."

I laughed. "I know everything when it comes to you."

"Not everything," Eden said. "Everyone confessed their heart out in there. Except me. And I don't feel good about it." Eden smiled. "I hate dramatics but the truth is I'm not feeling so hot. I'm sure no one else was."

"Technically, I didn't say anything either." I smirked.

"No I just want to get it over with," she said.

My smile faded. I nodded. "Okay."

"Um...okay. So I went to the party Fernando threw a

couple Fridays ago. It was great. Um Yusuf was there. He was drunk, I was drunk and I think I'm pregnant."

The world stopped. Time stopped. I couldn't process anything. Eden was babbling but I couldn't hear a word she said. It fell into a loud din. "He was just so...he was so beautiful and hazy. I just let him do whatever. And he was great. He was great. You think I'm an idiot? I-I wasn't thinking because I never do. Don't worry, Imma just go to planned parenthood and hand in what I earned the past 4 weeks for the abortion pill."

I felt myself falling into infinite darkness. I was reaching for something to hold on to but I couldn't grip anything. "I'm fine. I just wanted to tell somebody, you know?" She turned to head back inside but I grabbed her arm. "It's not fair," she rambled on. "I didn't tell him. I'm not gonna tell him. I'm not going to tell anyone." She laughed. "This is so embarrassing."

I stared down at my shoes. I opened my mouth but nothing came out. I gripped my head in anger.

"God we're a mess, aren't we?" Eden started to cry.

In a haste, I grabbed my wallet from my ebony dresser. Still distraught, I shoved the two of us out the window and onto the roof. I left the window open a crack. I headed over for the ladder wrapped in leafy vines hanging against Eden's house and climbed down to the grass. Eden followed me, unsure of what to do with herself. I grabbed her hand and the two of us took down the sidewalk.

We reached the town's CVS about five minutes later. I looked completely disheveled. My hair was unkempt and I had no shoes on my feet. I was wearing my tie-dye lime green and lemon yellow Mickey Mouse sweatshirt with red sweatpants. I scanned the aisles, not caring how Eden might have felt uncomfortable under my grip. And then I found it. I held up the First Response box and grabbed another one for good measure. We ran up to the counter. Ignoring the judgmental stare from the employee, I paid the 20 dollars and collected my change.

I pulled Eden into the CVS bathroom and shut the door behind us in the stall. I held the box out to her. "You have to pee on it."

Eden started crying. "I don't want to."

"You think this is a fucking joke?! You think I'm giving you a choice?! Pee on it now!"

She angrily ripped the box out of my hand and opened it up. She took the tester out. I turned around to give her some privacy. Once she finished washing up, I turned around and looked down at the test in the sink.

"How long does it say we have to wait?" I asked.

Eden checked the box. "One minute."

I nodded.

We waited for what seemed like an hour. "You look at it," she said. "I don't want to."

I looked down at it. My heart stopped. I remember looking at baby pictures of Eden when I was at her house. She had a huge toothless smile and her ginger coily hair seemed like it was extra curly. She was sitting beside Bleu and Todd. The twins were looking at her like she was the cutest creation they ever saw. Todd was pressing a kiss to Eden's cheek and Bleu was giving her a Barbie doll but her eyes were still focused on baby Eden. Unexpectedly, I hugged her. I squeezed her trying to get a sound to escape her mouth. "Congratulations," I whispered in her ear.

"No. No don't say that," she whispered back. "This was an accident."

"There are no accidents," I said.

Eden laughed but she choked on it. I quickly held onto her tighter. "It's okay. It's okay." I rubbed her back. She was shaking like a loose leaf. "You have a choice now. You can get rid of them or you can have them."

"Don't say them. They're not people yet."

"What do you want to do?" I asked her while staring at the wall.

"I don't know!" She shouted.

"Babies are hard." I smiled. "Babies are really hard to take care of. And we're just kids. But maybe your life was supposed to end up this way."

Eden rolled her eyes.

"Everything happens for a reason. And all the people that will judge you for what's happening to you right now, won't judge you in the future. You have friends and family that will help you. And you don't even have to have it."

She stared at me with a frightened look in her eyes.

"I don't want to do this," she said.

"Okay." I nodded. I rubbed her arms. "We have to tell. Your dad that you need to see a doctor-"

"I want it."

I froze. Her hazel eyes met with mine. "You do? Are you sure?"

"Yes," she nodded.

In utter shock, I covered my hands over my mouth. I wrapped my arms around her. "Congratulations!"

"Let's not tell anyone yet, please."

"Whatever you want!" I whacked her arm the way Avery does.

Eden shook her head at me then laughed lightly as her emotions rolled down her cheek in a single tear. She genuinely smiled.

Twenty

Let your soul stand cool and composed before a million universes.

- **Walt Whitman**

Monday was the first day back. We all had high hopes about our return to school. Apparently the principal had made an announcement about us on Friday, in an effort to alleviate the rumors as to why the one elevator was cordoned off. I was excited to be the talk of the school again ever since my freshman 'Save the World' phase but then I caught Jasmine, Eden and Quincy staring at a locker with a woebegone look on their face. Some students snorted withholding laughter as they passed by it. Stuart patted Quincy on the back.

"My gift to you," Stuart said quietly. "Don't ever kiss Bleu again." Stuart pushed her back. Quincy didn't waver her gaze on the word spray painted in yellow on her locker.

"You're such a coward," Eden said. "A pathetic coward. But you already knew that."

Stuart, on the verge of nearly responding, noticed me

and stopped grinning. He immediately walked around me avoiding eye contact.

Jealousy, I wrote out.

"No. Face it, Mercury!" Quincy exclaimed. Jasmine jumped. "You're wrong, okay? Not everyone is a faggot so drop it! Just drop it. Just...." Quincy began breathing heavily. I was worried she was gonna lose it again. "I'm not lucky like you. That's all I want. I just want to be happy and I can't be. Because then this shit happens to me." Her words echoed off the walls. We all stared at her wondering what she would do next. She placed her hands in her pockets and bit her lip, consistent puffs of air exhaled out of her nostrils. Then she acknowledged: "Being stuck in that elevator was the greatest thing that ever happened to me, Mercury. It's like my life stopped for a second so I could have time to scream and cry. But I was wrong to open up like that with that girl in there. It's like my problems collided so I could face the music all at once but it was too big for me to beat." She sighed. "I think I'm gonna go home now and try not to do anything stupid." She placed her hands on her hips. She rubbed her face, looking at the word one last time, then walked away.

The school was deserted at night. Scary, even. There wasn't one person walking through the hallways. I was spending the time I usually spend doing my homework and trying to ignore everything outside of my bedroom, scrubbing the word 'Dyke' off my friend's locker. Soft footsteps made their way over to where I was. I looked up and saw a familiar set of blonde curls. She sat down next to me. She gave a comforting smile. I began bawling overwhelmed by it all. I've been crying a lot lately. My dad thought it wouldn't be wise if I went back to school today but I had insisted on going.

"I didn't do this." She grabbed my notebook and handed it to me. I roughly swatted it out of her hand and listened to the pencil clink as it skid across the floor.

Bleu grabbed the sponge and tried to scrub the "k" off. I still wasn't able to control my emotions. I never can.

"Stop crying!" She scolded me. "I mean it, Mercury!"

I covered my mouth but I was still sniffling.

"Just calm down." She handed me the sponge. "I'm gonna search the janitor's closet for more sponges. Bleu scurried down the hall over to the janitor's closet.

The next morning, I told Quincy everything about what Bleu and I did for her last night and she beamed. "Bleu?" she asked confused.

I nodded.

"You put her up to this?"

I shook my head.

In AP chemistry, Quincy showed up late standing in front of me and Bleu's table instead of next to her lab partner, Stacey Rosenberg, who was glaring at Quincy from across the room. "Can I sit here for a second?"

I immediately got up and let Quincy take my seat next to Bleu.

"Oh god..." Bleu rolled her eyes.

"Thanks," Quincy said leaning into Bleu's ear. Bleu ignored her. She concentrated on finishing her lab report in front of her. "I didn't get to thank you in English class but thank you, Bleu."

Bleu continued to write.

"Bl-"

Bleu raised her hand. "Do you want us to hand this in?" She asked the teacher.

"Yes in the bin by the door."

"Thank you." Bleu got up and grabbed her work and placed it in the bin.

"Hey, Bleu." Quincy smiled at her as she took her seat next to her.

Bleu raised her eyebrows. "What? What now?"

"Oh nothing," Quincy said looking at Bleu's lips now. "Nothing it was just another thank you." A grin broke through me.

"How many times are you gonna say it?" Bleu asked.

"Until you say you're welcome.

"Mercury really scrubbed most of it off so-"

"Yeah but, she already said you're welcome."

"Well you're welcome," Bleu said.

"What?" Quincy cupped a hand around her ear. "Sorry I couldn't make out what you said."

"You're welcome."

"Huh?! What'd she say?"

"You're welcome you, aggravating b..." She hummed through the word with clenched teeth.

Stuart turned around. "What's going on?"

Quincy's smile faded. She looked straight ahead at the board. Bleu cleared her throat and looked down at her paper.

"Bleu?" Stuart said.

"Yup?"

"You okay?"

She looked up. "I'm fine why?"

Stuart looked at Quincy and then back over at Bleu.

"I'm fine," she said.

Stuart turned around to face the board.

Quincy stuck the finger up at Stuart behind his back for me. Bleu smirked and put Quincy's hand down. "Why are you still seeing him?" Quincy whispered to Bleu. Her eyes were still on the board. Bleu didn't answer. She just looked at her and then back at her paper again.

We all met up at the football game that night. I didn't want to go but Avery insisted because she loves watching our school fail at something. The school's football team hasn't won a single game since 2011. "Hey, Bleu!" Quincy waved.

Bleu's friend Cassidy snickered with Rachel.

"Oh shit sorry," Quincy looked at her hand confused. "It's like it has a mind of its own." That made Bleu smile.

I wrapped an arm around Quincy quickly pulling her away from Bleu and her friends' focal point. Avery rubbed Quincy's back sympathetically as they headed up the bleachers. "Don't bother. She's caught in the vortex of popularity."

"I don't even think she dumped S-t-u-a-r-t," Eden said.

"She told me they haven't slept together," Quincy stated.

"In the elevator?" Avery rubbed her chin.

"Yeah, you know, when all of you were *actually* asleep?"

Jasmine laughed loudly. "How'd you know we weren't asleep?"

"I heard you guys say you were gonna pretend to be asleep before I woke up."

"Mercury didn't sleep at all." I elbowed Eden's arm making her wince. Quincy stared at me.

"Oh look, look I think Stewart's about to make a touchdown!" We heard Cassidy shout.

We all watched as Stuart threw the football down across the white line and the crowd erupted into cheers. "Boo!" Quincy shouted. Avery, Jasmine and Eden joined in. Next thing I knew, the entire opposing team was booing. Quincy pretended to conduct the crowd.

"I'm gonna get a soda," she said. She roughly pulled my arm and wrapped hers around my shoulders. We jumped off the bleachers and headed over to the food stand. "So you heard everything?" she asked me. I nodded.

"Listen," she started. "I gotta tell you something."

I listened.

"It's dumb but Bleu and I kissed again the day before we got stuck in that elevator."

I was about to write that I knew but she held her hand over mine.

"Wait just listen. It was late. I walked back to the field because I left my cleats on the sidewalk where we leave our water."

I stared at her. This story was already sounding different than the other one.

Quincy cleared her throat when I didn't react. "I saw a soccer ball on the field but I wasn't wearing my cleats while I was playing so I was prone to slipping, mind you. Then Bleu showed up. She told me that she followed me there. She was apologizing and apologizing for the race thing then I started apologizing for the mom thing. We were both babbling. It didn't make any sense. It was gibberish. I kicked the ball when we stopped and I fell. Instead of laughing, she helped me up but then she slipped and fell on me. She stared at me for like a minute before she leaned down and kissed me. And she kissed me. And she kissed me." Quincy laughed looking

167

over at the bleachers. "And kissed me so I kissed her. We made out for like ten minutes." She shrugged with a smile. I was completely stunned.

I couldn't figure out what I was more impressed by: Bleu's ability to give a strong composed lie or the fact that Quincy would admit this to me. I started to think about Bleu and Quincy's relationship in the elevator. "The entire ordeal was awkward not being able to talk about it until a certain point, which I'm sure you heard." I nodded still reeling from what she shared with me. "So," she said. She removed her arm and stopped walking so I could face her. "Do you think she likes me?"

There is a 90 percent chance she does.

"Hey, that's pretty good."

It is.

"I'm not going to do anything, though. Unless I wanna embarrass the crap outta myself and her. And I got a good thing going with Lily." Quincy was ordering a hot dog when Bleu came up behind her and tapped her on the shoulder. She jumped. "Oh shit it's you."

"You can, like, talk to me," Bleu said. Her hoop earrings dangled as she spoke.

"Oh." Quincy nodded. She looked around. "Uh are you sure?"

"Yeah, Quincy," she said in aggravation.

100 percent chance she does.

Quincy snorted. Bleu pointed towards my notebook. "What does that mean?"

Quincy waved it off, smiled weakly. "No thanks to the talking thing," she said. "I don't want your friends laughing at me again."

Bleu's eyes filled with an intense amount of desire as she stared at Quincy. "Quincy, I won't let them laugh at you."

"It's okay, Bleu." She smiled. "Really. I'm not offended." Quincy subtly motioned behind her with her hot dog. "Here comes one of them now." I turned my head and saw Rachel coming over to us. "I should go," Quincy said nearly tripping over something. "Enjoy the game, alright?" She quickly took off, repeatedly colliding her palm against her forehead.

"What was that about?" Rachel asked. "You just left and didn't say anything."

"Its nothing." Bleu scratched her head. "I wanted a slice of pizza."

"I came for Lays. Do they have those?"

"Yeah right there." Bleu pointed. "You can cut me."

"Great." Rachel glanced over at me. "Yes? Need something?"

I blew a raspberry in her face and I left how I usually leave: without saying a word.

Twenty-one

Listen, you hear it? - - Carpe - - hear it? - - Carpe, carpe diem, seize the day, boys. Make your lives extraordinary.

- **Dead Poets Society (1989)**

Avery came out of her house and to the pier with her hair up in a high bun wearing a pink t-shirt and ripped faded light blue jeans. "I'm here. What's up?" She said as she sat close to me. Her knees knocked against mine.

"Thank you."

"For what?"

"For saving my life," I said. "I trusted you before I knew your name."

"I didn't do anything. It was William."

"It was you," I said.

Avery pressed her lips to my rose pink hair and left them there. "Promise me you won't ever cover your mouth again," she muffled.

"I promise."

Avery leaned in to kiss me but I leaned back. "My dad owns the masonry building on 2nd street. He works for this theatrical company and he managed to buy that building out so he's the owner. It's intimidatingly huge and I never really wanted to go inside because I'm not really into performing arts. Mirrors scare me because I hate looking at myself and I hate my fear. I'm kind of afraid he'll want me to join." Avery was quietly listening as I continued: "He attended Juilliard for piano and singing but he didn't make much money starting out so he joined this company that helps seek all kinds of creative talent for old and new aspiring artists. The company is very successful. It's a much bigger deal than I'm making it out to be. A lot of that money is gonna help me pay for college. The building is open from 9am to 8pm but sometimes the janitor takes a nap and he leaves the door unlocked." I exhaled.

Avery nodded seemingly interested. She intertwined our dangling legs swinging back and forth between the ocean and sky.

I smiled and scratched my arm.

Avery snorted. "And? Is their a point?"

"I watch you dance there."

Avery's smile faded into the sea breeze. "Are you freakn' kidding me? People watch me?"

"Just me," I said.

"You pervert!" She swatted my tricep.

"How?!" I said trying not to giggle.

"I do some other shit in there. Some weird shit!"

"I know."

"Are you like a stalker or something?!"

"Yeah that's it. You're very entertaining."

"God. You... ugh. You're a loon. What's the point of watching me everyday if I'm not even a good dancer?"

"Why do we open the blinds every morning if we're just gonna end up closing them again?"

"I don't know. Those questions don't have the same answer."

"Sure they do. To see beauty."

"Ewww!"

"I wasn't trying to be cheesy, Avery. I was being honest."

"Whatever," she rested her chin on the back of her hand. "Say that again."

"What?"

She stared at me as if I already knew. I scoffed and poked her side with my finger. Then we were quiet for a while, listening to the waves. I felt like I could sit here for the rest of my life with Avery. The moon was reflecting off her silky red hair. Shimmering like dancing glitter the way it did on the ocean. "Just once," Avery begged timidly barely above a whisper.

"Avery," I said slowly.

Avery rolled her eyes back. "Jesus H."

"Who's the loon now?"

"Us." Avery looked over at me. Her luminous irises were blinding my thoughts. I love her.

"How do you do that dance you always do?" I asked. "The one where its like a cross between a bird trying to fly and a constipated monkey."

"Oh you mean…?" She stood up and did it.

"Yeah." I stood up and tried to do it.

"Something like that. You'll get the hang of it."

Offended, I picked her up ignoring her loud boisterous protests and jumped with her into the dark blue glittery water with our only worry being hoping we remembered how to swim and not about the future.

"Maybe this wasn't a good idea," I said staring across our booth at Mary's diner.

"Hey you can talk in here," Avery pointed out.

"Oh yeah."

"And don't worry, this was a collaborative idea, let's have fun."

I smiled. "Okay." We thought it would be a good idea for the six of us to get together since it was so easy to talk to one another in the elevator. Despite the fighting, starvation, crying and awkward moments, that should have traumatized us, I had a pretty good time. Maybe even Bleu would show up.

Quincy strolled up to our booth. She was dressed in the forest green apron with "Mary's Diner" stitched on it. She took a seat next to Avery. "Hey guys."

"Hey," said Avery.

"Hi," I said.

Quincy shook her head side to side. She reached over the table to ruffle my pink hair. "Man, I'll never get used to that talking thing."

Eden took a seat next to me. She was dressed in the same apron as Quincy. She drummed her hands on the table. "Did you hear?"

"Hear what?"

"Bleu dumped Stuart today."

I looked over at Avery mid-chuckle.

"Good," Avery said. "That was long overdue."

"No, guys. She poured soup on the guy's head," Eden laughed but then she cleared her throat. "She got suspended, though. She gave him like first degree burns."

"Good," Avery repeated. "That was long overdue."

"I just feel bad she got suspended for such a humble redefining act," said Eden.

"Yeah that sucks. How long is she suspended for?"

"Two days," Eden said.

We all winced in unison.

"I know." She stood up. "I gotta get back to work. Later."

"So do I," Quincy said. "I only have two tables tonight, though. Should be finished soon."

Avery nodded. She rubbed her chin. "You like this job?" Avery asked.

Quincy shrugged. "Keeps me busy, gives me money, why not? Sure I like this job."

"How's Lily?" I asked to change the subject.

"Oh I broke up with her." So much for that.

"What? Why?"

"I told her who I was with when I was stuck in the elevator and she kind of hates everyone that was in the elevator."

"Aww you dumped her for us." Avery pouted her lips with a hidden smile. "How sweet."

"Yeah," Quincy said. "She was also kind of mean."

"Oh really?!" I gasped. "God, Lily? No! I don't believe it for a second."

Avery howled with laughter.

"What's your deal?" Quincy asked slightly amused. "You don't like her?"

"She told me off when I was with Bleu. I couldn't even say anything."

"You have many looks. She probably took offense to one of them."

"When were you with Bleu?" Avery turned her gaze toward me. Her laughter came to an end.

"They were having a confidential talk," Quincy said. Clearly Avery was taking this the wrong way. I wanted to strangle Quincy.

"About what?" Avery asked.

"I-I'll tell you later," I said.

The bell above the door chimed and Bleu stepped into the diner. She was wearing a grey pea coat, large silver hoop earrings and had a new buzz cut. She spotted us and came over to sit next to me. She looked amazing. I couldn't take my eyes off her.

Avery was just as stunned. "Wow. Bleu."

Quincy's mouth hung open looking her over. "Woah."

"What?" Bleu asked. Her face flushed like crimson red wine was poured into her cheeks.

"Nothing," Quincy said.

"My hair was all in my face so-"

"Right," Quincy said. "I knew that. I mean, I didn't but that could be such a hassle. Hair." Quincy nervously bounced her knee up and down while staring at her fingers on the table.

"Can I touch it?" I asked. Avery kicked me under the table but I ignored her.

"Sure," Bleu said.

I delicately ran my fingers through the back of her hair. Blonde fuzz outlined my fingertips one after the other.

"How does it feel?" Avery asked bitterly.

"Soft," I gently snuck my hand out and rested my arm behind her. "Nice." I felt two pairs of feet kick me that time.

"Thanks." Bleu glanced at Quincy before back at the

menu on the table. You could cut through the tension in the booth with a knife.

"I have to use the bathroom." I said and obnoxiously climbed over Bleu.

"Me, too." Avery said bumping into Quincy on her way out. "I have to take a shit. I'll be right back." I headed into the women's restroom and into the handicap stall only to have Avery follow me in. Avery broke into hysterics. "We're so evil. I can't believe we just left them there. What do you think they're doing."

"Trying not to tell each other," I said simply.

"Tell each other what?" She pushed her fiery hair behind her ear.

I smiled. "They're in looooove," I sang.

Avery cocked her head. "You think they're in love?" She asked slowly almost as if she were sounding out the words.

"Yeah."

"You're a love expert?" I thought back to the night she told me she loved me and I didn't believe her. For the first time in a while, I regretted talking. "So you were right about me not being in love with you?"

"I don't think I'd be able to identify love that was directed towards me." That sounded smart, I assured myself. Let's stick with that.

"Oh I see." She chuckled lightly. No you don't, you're infuriated, I thought to myself. But I nodded. Then I directed my attention to my Air Jordans. "So you think they love each other, huh?"

I glanced up. I gave out an artificial laugh. And it wasn't even a good one. "They both dumped who they were seeing."

Avery gave out a laugh, too. Awkward silence. "Let's go back, then," she said."

"Uh let's not."

"It's beginning to smell in here, girl."

"Yeah."

Avery smiled. "So we should... go." She motioned for the door.

"No." I'm going to tell her. I can do it. It's like ripping a bandage off.

"Why?"

"We haven't been in here long enough," I said.

"I have," she countered. She bit her bottom lip and unlocked the stall door. Just tell her! I laughed at my own expense.

"It's really hot in here," I said.

"Listen um I know we're not exclusive, so I thought I'd kick it with this guy next weekend if it's cool with you."

I smiled. I felt like a pathetic pumpkin on Halloween: hollow. All my insides were carved out only for my guts to be thrown away in the trash.

Avery rolled her eyes playfully. "Aren't you gonna say something?"

"No, yeah. It's fine. It's cool."

"Cool, he's really nice." Avery winked. "He has a pilot license."

"He can fly?" I asked in a whisper. She's stealing my voice away from me.

She smiled like a cheshire cat. "Yeah, he can fly."

"Can't compete with that."

"No, Mercury. You don't have to compete with anything."

I had no idea I said that last bit aloud. I felt claustrophobic. "We should get back now." I laughed.

"Thank you." She smiled and followed me out. When we were heading back over to the table, I started feeling like I was still so far from it. Like walking on stars. Expecting to end up somewhere but everything is pitch black and looks the same. Bleu was laughing at something Quincy said when we got there. They looked so happy and I instantly became jealous.

"We still haven't ordered yet," Avery mentioned.

"Oh that's right I'm your server," Quincy said. She took a pencil out of her apron.

I raised my hands up in the air. "Perfect." I closed in next to Bleu.

Quincy laughed. "Quiet." She stood up to let Avery in. "What do you want?"

"I'm not hungry," Bleu said.

"Of course you're not."

Avery and I froze waiting for Bleu to blow up into smithereens. She frowned with confusion. "What does that mean?"

"Nothing," Quincy said quickly. She shook her head fervently.

"Good answer," Avery said.

Bleu furrowed her eyebrows. "No, I wanna know."

"You're small and skinny," Quincy said. "This food is fattening. You don't look like the kind of person to consume fattening things."

"I eat fattening things." Bleu folded her arms over her chest and leaned back. "Get me a strawberry shake."

"Okay." Quincy scribbled it down. Her pink tongue was poking out in concentration.

"Cheeseburger," Avery said.

"Can I have a hamburger?" I asked. Avery didn't look at me. "I'll have a sprite, too," I added.

"Water, please," Avery said.

"Got it. I'll be right back." Quincy headed towards the bustling kitchen. Bleu reached over me and took hold of Quincy's hand and pulled her back to her view.

"Yes?"

"I was just wondering," she said. "What do you have a tattoo of?"

"You really wanna know?"

Bleu nodded.

Quincy looked pleased. "Carpe Diem."

"Interesting. Seize the day. Have you seen Dead Poet's Society?"

"It's my favorite movie."

"Poetry, beauty, romance, love, these are what we stay alive for."

Quincy nodded absentmindedly stunned.

"I love that movie." She released her hand.

Quincy gulped and left.

Avery laughed. "That wasn't nice."

I released the laugh I was holding in. I clapped slowly. Bleu smirked at the two of us. "Why?"

"She's working," I said.

"So I was just quoting a line from the movie? I've seen it fifty-two times."

"No you were flirting," I corrected.

"I'm not gay. How many times do I have to repeat myself."

"We didn't say you were," Avery and I said together.

"I'm not."

"Whatever," Avery said. "O captain, my captain."

Jasmine quickly barged in through the front door in a complete disarray. The bell above the door chimed violently. "Hey guys. Sorry I'm late." Jasmine paused. "Bleu, you showed up?"

"Yeah why?"

"Well after everything that happened today, I didn't think your dad would even let you out of the house. And your hair." She tilted her head while she was unbuttoning her baby blue pea coat. She smiled. "I love it."

"Thanks." Bleu blushed.

Jasmine scooted beside Avery.

"Where were you?" Avery pried.

"Uh Jack dropped me off at my house," Jasmine replied. "My family wasn't having it."

"Not even Sarafina?" I asked.

Jasmine laughed. "Not even Sarafina."

"What happened to Jack?"

"My dad cursed him out in Arabic then he went home. He says he's fine."

"Atta boy."

Avery grinned. "He's probably crying right now."

Jasmine nodded. "Yeah, undoubtedly."

Quincy came back with her black tray filled with icy cold beverages. "Here ya go." She placed all the drinks down onto the table. "Hey, Jas. Want something to drink?"

"Hey. Uh just water for now please. I'm stuffed."

"You got it." Quincy left.

Bleu raised her cup. "To being out of those four walls. Cheers." The three of us clinked our cups together before we drank.

"Back to you, Bleu," Jasmine said. "How are you like... here?"

Bleu sat up straighter. "My dad was proud of me when I told him everything. I think he still feels bad about my eye."

"Your dad did that?!" Avery asked pointing to the purple bruise under Bleu's eye.

"It was a justifiable accident. I promise you." She explained what happened.

"Ah."

"After I told him what really happened with Mercury and everything, I told him I wanted a haircut."

"Hey. I'm done. Finito!" Eden sat beside me and wiped her forehead off with a napkin. She frowned at me. "What's wrong?"

"Nothing?" I said confused.

Eden narrowed her eyes. I leaned away from her.

"She looks fine to me," said Bleu.

"Please," Eden said holding her hand up. "I've known her my whole life."

"So have I."

"Not the way I have," she said still staring at me.

"I'm okay, really," I lied. Even I didn't believe that.

Eden pulled me closer and cupped a hand around my ear. She leaned in and whispered, "I know you're lying, idiot. We'll deal with this later."

I nodded. I could sense Avery's lasers cutting me open.

"I can't believe our piss is in a large puddle at the bottom of the school elevator," Jasmine blurted out randomly. Everyone laughed at that.

Quincy put our burgers and fries down and took a seat next to Jasmine. She rested her elbows on the table, batted her eyelashes and rested her chin on her intertwined fingers. "My shift is over." She glanced around at all of us. "What'd I miss?"

I folded my arms and paced the entrance of the diner. The street was quiet and starkly deserted. A biting cold chill whipped at my face everytime I swiveled my body to the side Avery was standing on. She was putting on her brown bulky coat staring at me quizzically. "Want me to walk you home?" Avery asked me.

"Nah I'm cool. I'm gonna-" I pointed behind me. "Take a walk."

Avery stared at me for a few more seconds. "Are you okay?"

"Don't listen to Eden. I'm fine."

Avery nodded reluctantly and turned to walk home. She looked back at me. She made out a small smile before continuing her stride. Bleu and Quincy were talking to one another by the lamppost but they weren't aware of my presence. I headed over to the brick wall at the next corner to make my way home but I was able to hear what they were saying clearly from there. I stood on the damp ground hidden and overcast by a shadow made by the dim lamp light. Bleu and Quincy made their way over to the intersection and were now lying in the middle of the street. Bleu slowly closed her eyes.

"What if we get run over?" Quincy asked.

"We won't." A smile tugged at Bleu's lips. She was breathing heavily.

"Are you sure?"

Bleu nodded.

"Well I'll pull you up if I see a car."

"Okay."

Quincy looked up. "Car!"

Bleu quickly jumped up making Quincy chuckle. Bleu pulled Quincy up. "Point taken."

"I don't see any cars, though. It's really odd."

"There's never any cars down this street this late."

Quincy stepped closer to her. "You must come here a lot"

Bleu nodded. "I do to think." She stepped away as she spoke to hide from the light casting on her. "I think that's why I'm so crazy. I'm alone with my thoughts too often. And it's usually because I think the world is after me."

"Me, too."

Me, three, I thought.

"But it's just all in our head," Bleu continued. "We're dots. That's why I don't get why we praise people so much. We're all just tiny dots that will eventually die out. And the worst part is when we're all dead, we won't be able to regret the things we've done throughout our entire lifetime. We die with no regrets."

"What are you doing for the rest of your life?" Quincy asked.

"Letting the chips fall where they may." I watched as Bleu slinked walked away from Quincy and onto the sidewalk not too far from where I stood. "It's late. I should really get home."

"Oh okay." Quincy followed her to the sidewalk before stopping. "See you at school Monday, kid."

"Bye," Bleu said.

Quincy smiled and played with a rock on the sidewalk.

"You're staying out here alone?" Bleu asked.

Quincy shrugged. Her thick wispy hair glowed like a halo under the lamppost. "I really love the quiet."

"As do I."

Quincy planted herself down on the edge of the sidewalk. "We seem to have a lot in common."

Bleu hesitantly kneeled down beside her. Quincy kicked a rock with her foot into the road. It rolled into the street with the ongoing apprehension and unnecessary tension.

"Are you still into June Matthews?" Bleu asked the sky.

"A little bit."

"She's nice. I've been to her house. It's massive. It has three bathrooms and four bedrooms. Uh let's see. A guest area, a living room, two dining rooms, a whole room for the pool table, a pool, and a great backyard."

"Wow," Quincy said.

"Yeah. It's intense."

"How many times have you been there?" Quincy wiggled her eyebrows.

"Once," Bleu smirked. "For her sixteenth birthday party."

"Ah." Quincy leaned her chin against her knees. "Sounds like fun."

"Yeah she's nice." The quiet air thickened. Bleu and Quincy accidentally met each other's eyes when they looked over at each other. They jerked their heads away simultaneously.

Absolute silence. The air became thick enough to hold anything in it.

"Let's cut the crap now." Quincy cackled. She stood up and rested back against the lamppost to look down at Bleu. Unable to withstand her gaze she gripped the lamppost and turned to look in the opposite direction. "You're hotter than June Matthews. On a scale of 1-10, she's a 9 and you're like an 87. I just didn't want to embarrass you in the fucking elevator that's all." She cleared her throat.

Bleu went as scarlet as Avery's hair. "If I sat next to you in math, and June was stuck in the elevator with you," she whispered. "Would you say the same things you said about her about me?"

"I wouldn't feel the need to."

"That's what I thought," Bleu scoffed. "You wouldn't even mention me."

"I wouldn't say it because I don't need to make June jealous," she said to an empty road.

"You were trying to make me jealous? Why? That's so selfish. You know how insecure I can be."

"Because...I don't know if you like me, Bleu! You're so beautiful and I like you more than anything but it's like all you do is try to make my life so hard. It's been annoying to have feelings for you for this long so I'm just gonna move on now. You're not worth all this trouble anymore." She kicked a rock into the road again.

"Do you think I would be spending my entire Friday night with you if I didn't like you?" She stood up tears racing from her eyes. "Of course I like you, I'm in love with you." Bleu froze.

Quincy didn't speak but she clamped a hand over her

185

mouth. Her eyes were already as red as Avery's clothes. As red as Avery's lips. Her eyes welled with tears.

Bleu nearly screamed. "Oh my god. I'm going home."

"Wait, Bleu."

"No I'm leaving," her voice cracked.

"I love you, too." Quincy smiled. "You're the only bitch that ever talks to me. And you're not a bitch."

"I have to go."

"Okay," Quincy said trying not to smile. She pressed her palms to her cheeks.

"Where's my lighter?" Bleu fervently patted her pockets.

It was lying in front of Quincy's feet. Quincy quickly snatched it up off the ground.

"Give it to me." Bleu put her shaky hand out.

"You shouldn't be smoking."

"Give it to me!"

"Okay I will." She put it behind her back, backing away from Bleu. "You just have to get it."

"No."

"Fine."

"Quincy!"

"Bleu!"

Bleu screamed.

And Quincy made the largest smile in the world.

Bleu reached for it behind Quincy's back and Quincy quickly kissed her on her cheek. She tried to get in again and Quincy kissed her other cheek. "I love you."

Bleu roughly backed Quincy into a lamppost and slammed her mouth onto hers. Quincy tried to speak but Bleu kissed her again making her eyes fly out of her head. Quincy erupted into a laughing fit. She chucked the lighter and Bleu didn't budge. Smoking is bad for you.

Twenty two

So there's no winning. There's no winning. You just have to be happy with who you are.

- **Sir Robert Bryson Hall II**

A girl keeps smiling at me. She's talking to a woman about a book and she's smiling at me behind the bookshelf. She looked like she was half Asian and half white. She had inky black hair, two small braids dangling in front of her face while the rest is held up in the back in a ponytail. She had a black choker around her neck and an orange T-shirt with the word 'Backwards Living' spelled backwards. I honestly just want to finish this poetry book I picked up. I perused the book and read a poem about love and roses that automatically made me think about-

"Hi. I just wanted to tell you I like your hair."

"Oh," I said startled. "Thank you. I appreciate it." Avery, sitting in front of me, glanced up from her novel.

"I love that book. I love poetry."

"You do? Of course you do, you work here."

The girl giggled. "I actually don't like the manga."

"Manga is iffy. Graphic novels are cool, though."

"Yeah, graphic novels are cool," she agreed. "There was one, I think about a superhero who has the power to be invisible but if you pour alcohol on him he's doomed, kinda like his kryptonite."

"Can you imagine?" I started laughing. I looked over at Avery who wasn't laughing and then back at the girl. "Being caught at the wrong time doing some embarrassing act and then smelling like beer. I got one: the guy goes to work completely naked to get his shit done but some woman, probably stressed out of her mind, brings a coffee cup filled with scotch in it and bumps into him by accident as she passes by him."

The girl and I were dying with laughter. I held out my hand. "I'm Mercury. This is Avery."

"Lucy." We shook hands. "Come on I'll show you the book."

"Sweet," I said. "I'll be back, Avery."

"Take your time," Avery insisted.

Lucy and I went up to the top floor of the bookstore. She stopped at the second bookshelf and scanned the whole thing.

"I bet you've read all of these, huh?" I asked. I folded my arms, viewing all the books on the shelf.

Lucy turned around to face me. She was fiddling with a thread poking out of the hem of her orange t-shirt. "Are you gay?" She asked. I instantaneously started laughing at the presumptuousness. "I'm sorry. That was-you don't have to answer."

"No it's fine. I am." I twisted my body side to side like an anomalous child. "Are...you?"

"Yeah."

"Okay."

"There's this coffee place near here and they're having this poetry reading thing. Do yo-"

"Yeah." My eyes widened. "Sorry you can finish."

She laughed. "No, I want you to come with me. I just met you but I think you're sweet."

"Sweet," I said. "I'd love to come."

"You're not dating that girl are you? The one you were with."

I laughed. "No we're just friends." It's been three weeks, almost a month, since the elevator incident. I've been able to open up more and not just with certain people. It's brought my self esteem up at least ten percent. I've been thinking that maybe there is more to life than just being born, breathing for a bit, and then dying. Bleu's out with Quincy now, Jasmine's out with Jack, Zachariah broke up with Sydney and Eden told her family about the baby. She even told Yusuf who, when he found out, got on his knees and hugged her stomach for five minutes. She thought her father would never speak to her again but he hasn't left her side. I've been talking to Eden a lot lately. She's been looking a lot healthier and ethereal. The scars and cuts on her arm are fading away with the past. Avery's the same. She still hangs out with the same people. She still sleeps around. I'm over it.

We walked in silence on our way home from the book store with a foot of space between us.

"She asked you out?" Avery asked bluntly.

I smirked. "Yeah."

"She was pretty."

I nodded. "She was cool."

Avery stopped walking. "I think I'm jealous of her."

189

I asked myself if I should be happy about that because I was. "Why do you think that?" I asked.

"I have all the symptoms."

"Just fight it then."

"Okay." Avery continued walking. "Are you gonna have sex with her?"

Normally, I would laugh but I became frustrated. "What?" I asked.

"I just want to know," she said.

"I'm not going to tell you."

"Okay."

I gave a single nod. She stopped walking again. "Do you hate me?"

The second I was about to give an answer, a yellow car rolled up beside Avery. "Hey, Avery! Going to Jackson's party?"

"Uh maybe. That's tonight already?"

"Yeah?!" A girl with short blue hair said. She was halfway out the passenger seat window looking at Avery. "I've been texting you all day about it."

"Right." Avery snorted.

The girl laughed. "We'll see you."

"See you." We watched them drive off.

"Jackson's the one with the pilot license?" I asked.

"No that's Andrew."

"Oh." I rolled my eyes when I continued my stride. "Hey, I forgot to ask you what's your tattoo?"

Avery shook her head. "It's no Carpe Diem."

"Is it stupid?"

"It's really stupid."

I laughed. "What is it?"

"I'm not gonna tell you yet."

"I have to earn it?"

She nodded.

"Okay." We stopped in front of my house. I headed up the white wooden porch steps and up to my front door. "See ya."

"I'm still jealous of her," Avery said smiling widely. She rested her chin on the newel post of the banister. "She's classy. She's prettier than me. She's probably smarter than me since she works at a bookstore."

"She doesn't fly," I said mimicking her smile.

"She can jump," Avery argued. "Jumping; you're in the air and then you land."

"That's a positive approach."

"It's true."

"Bye, Avery." Goodbye, Avery.

"Bye, Mercury."

"Have fun at the party." I went inside before I could notice her expression.

-

I woke up in the middle of the night to a harsh thump on my stomach. I blinked my eyes open and there she was on top of me. I opened my mouth to scream but Avery instantly covered my mouth with the palm of her hand. "You left the window open," she explained.

"Get out," I ordered.

"No."

I pushed myself up. "Avery."

"No, Mercury." She darted her dull green eyes back and forth looking at the two of mine. "I love you. I love you so much." She broke into tears. "I'm sorry for everything I've done."

I watched her cry. She still seemed like she wasn't here to me. It almost felt like I was watching a dramatic television show she was starring in or she was a faulty hologram. I rested my forehead against hers and rubbed Avery's temples.

Avery's crying died down and she kept sniffling.

"I won't go on the date," I said.

"No, you should."

"I won't go," I said laughing. "I don't even want to go."

Avery took a breath trying not to erupt into tears again. "She's so pretty." I shushed her until it was evident that she was calm. "I know you were gonna tell me you loved me in the stall." That made her cry even louder. "I'm sorry." My heart started beating out of my chest. It was thumping louder than ever but I didn't care. I laughed but then I started to cry. I gripped Avery's head tighter and pressed my lips to hers. I hungrily pressed rough kisses all over Avery.

"I don't want you to see anyone anymore," I said louder than I hoped. "But you can do whatever you want. I just don't like it when you cry. I love you and I don't like seeing you cry."

"I love you and I don't like seeing you cry either," Avery said.

"I'm only crying 'cause you are."

"On the count of three," she choked out. "We stop. 1-2-3."

We were quiet for a sweet solid second before the two of us busted out laughing. I flew back on the bed giggling. Avery climbed over me and wiped my eyes.

"Please show me your tattoo," I begged.

"I won't see anyone anymore," she said.

We said the two phrases at the same time making us giggle again.

"That's good," I said first.

"It's a dinosaur," Avery said.

"No it's not."

"It is." Avery positioned herself beside me and propped herself up on her elbow. She pulled her pants down and showed me a cute green cartoon T-rex tattoo on her left thigh.

"I like it."

"You hate it."

"I'll name it."

"Okay..."

"Mercuryasaurus Rex."

"Why does it have to be named after you?"

"Because I adopted it. Him."

"It's a girl, actually." She rolled her eyes. "Shows how much you know."

"Oh that's right," I said still staring at it. I pointed towards a figure on Mercurysaurus. "I think I see a pink bow. Don't see many of those in Jurassic Park."

"Boy dinosaurs can wear pink bows," she said matter-of-factly.

"You're right." I smiled at her with wide eyes. She looked over at me and laughed.

"Told you it was stupid."

"She's beautiful," I told her. "It's no Carpe Diem. It's better than Carpe Diem."

Avery looked up at me with a genuine smile.

Printed in the United States
By Bookmasters